YO-AWG-964

Australian Showdown

"I'm gonna give you a beating, Adams, and the only way you can avoid it is to shoot an unarmed man—with witnesses."

"Well, since there's hardly any law out here, Pickett, I don't think that would be a problem," Clint said, and for a moment he saw uncertainty in Pickett's eyes. However, when he dropped his gunbelt to the floor the man's eyes hardened once again.

"Now that's a mistake," Pickett said. "You should have killed me."

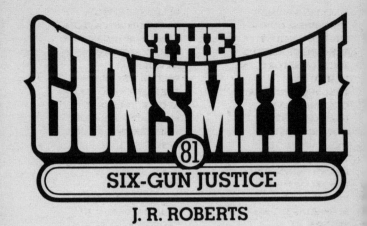

THE GUNSMITH

81

SIX-GUN JUSTICE

J. R. ROBERTS

J
JOVE BOOKS, NEW YORK

THE GUNSMITH #81: SIX-GUN JUSTICE

A Jove book / published by arrangement with
the author

PRINTING HISTORY
Jove edition / September 1988

All rights reserved.
Copyright © 1988 by Robert J. Randisi.
This book may not be reproduced in whole or in part,
by mimeograph or any other means, without permission.
For information address: The Berkley Publishing Group,
200 Madison Avenue, New York, New York 10016.

ISBN: 0-515-09709-8

Jove books are published by The Berkley Publishing Group,
200 Madison Avenue, New York, New York 10016.
The name ''Jove'' and the ''J'' logo
are trademarks belonging to Jove Publications, Inc.

PRINTED IN THE UNITED STATES OF AMERICA

10 9 8 7 6 5 4 3 2 1

SIX-GUN JUSTICE

ONE

The man seated across the poker table from Clint Adams was the big winner of the night—so far. In fact, from what Clint had learned, the man had been winning big all week.

There were four other players at the table, and they were all losing. Clint was holding his own, but in a game this size he'd almost rather have been losing. Playing high-stakes poker for four hours with nothing to show for it was like wasting four hours.

The big winner's name was Thomas Ross. The other players were Lawrence Black, John Healy, Jerry Lutz, and Bob McCoy. Clint did not know what any of these gentlemen did for a living. There was little or no small talk during the game, which was just as well. All the players—including himself—took this caliber of poker very seriously, and it commanded all of their attention.

Clint had been in San Francisco a week and had done fairly well at the casinos in Portsmouth Square. His success had obviously not gone unnoticed, because as soon as a chair had opened up at this private game, he had been approached to fill it.

He had jumped at the chance. After all, this was what he had come to San Francisco to do: gamble, drink, and meet some women. Forget some of the things that had happened over the past few months, most notably his recent experiences with a man named Johnny Robak.[1]

Through a series of circumstances, Clint had gone down under a bullet from Robak's gun, and he had found out what life would be like if he weren't the Gunsmith anymore.

He hadn't liked it, and now he was confused. He'd always hated the rep he carried, but now he knew what would happen if he lost it.

Instead of thinking about it, he decided to come to San Francisco and lose himself in everything it had to offer.

Most notably gambling . . . and women.

More specifically poker . . . and Delinda Griffin.

Thomas was dealing, and Clint let all five cards fall before he picked them up.

The game was draw, and all that was needed to open was the guts to do so.

To Clint's right sat Black and Healy, to his left Lutz and McCoy.

---

1. THE GUNSMITH #80: WHEN LEGENDS DIE

Clint spread his cards and found himself looking at a pat hand, an ace high, heart flush.

Black passed, but Healy opened. He'd done so a couple of times and had tried to steal the pot by calling a pat hand. On both occasions, it had been Thomas who had beaten him, and on neither occasion had he had a truly pat hand. He stood with three of a kind once, and two pair once.

"A hundred," Healy said.

"Call," Clint said, because he wanted to keep as many of the players in as possible. They'd call Healy as a matter of course, but if he raised, they'd take him seriously.

A bet went around to Ross, who raised.

"Up a hundred."

Clint was convinced that it was just a bump to build the pot. The man was making the mistake a lot of gamblers made, even the better ones. He was playing his luck. He had nothing, but he did have a promising hand, and he was raising on it.

Of course, it was that kind of play that usually ended up beating a pat hand. Somebody keeping two high cards or drawing to a flush and making it, instead of going out, as he should have—and might have—had his luck not been running hot.

"Cards?" Ross asked.

Black drew three and Healy stood pat, as Clint had suspected he would.

When Ross looked at Clint, Clint said, "I'll play these."

Everyone had looked resigned when Healy stood pat, but now they perked up and looked interested.

"Will you, now?" Ross said. "This could get interesting."

Lutz drew a card and McCoy asked for three.

"The dealer takes three," Ross said, confirming what Clint

had thought after having observed the man's play. Ross had probably raised on a high pair, depending on his luck to improve his hand.

"You opened, Mr. Healy," Ross said. The man seemed to have an excellent memory for names, producing the proper one with seemingly no effort.

Whatever Healy had, he had to bet or ruin his play.

"Two hundred," Healy said, eyeing Clint.

"Call," Clint said, counting out his chips, "and up two-fifty."

"That's it," Lutz said, dropping his cards to the table.

"I'll call," said McCoy, "only because it promises to be the most interesting hand of the night."

"And the most expensive," Ross said. "I'll call, and raise five hundred."

Black groaned and folded.

"Call," Healy said tightly.

"Call," Clint said, "and raise five hundred."

If he'd thought about it more he might not have raised, but the hand he held deserved to be played, notwithstanding the luck Ross had been exhibiting. The odds were high on turning a pair into a full house or four of a kind, and that's what it would take to beat Clint. He had to play against what he thought Ross's *cards* were, and not the man's luck.

"Well," McCoy said, putting his cards down, "it was expensive, wasn't it?"

"And it's not over yet," Ross said.

He couldn't raise, Clint thought, not unless he had truly filled up.

"I raise a thousand."

That put it to Healy, who had stayed pat for the third time.

"Healy?" Ross said. "What's your pat hand say to that?"

"I call," Healy said, glumly. He must have really had a pat hand this time and couldn't bring himself to fold it.

"And pat hand number two?" Ross asked.

No, Clint thought, he wouldn't back away from Ross's luck. If he did he'd never forgive himself—win or lose.

"Call and raise, Ross."

"Well," Ross said, "I guess you've got it," and folded his hand.

All eyes fell on Healy, who was staring at Ross.

"Healy?" Clint said.

Healy jerked his eyes away from Ross and looked at Clint.

"Call, raise, or fold," Ross said, still speaking as the dealer.

"I call," Healy said. He threw in his chips and spread his cards. He'd had a high club straight, to the ace, right from the deal.

"He really had a pat hand this time," Ross said.

"So do I," Clint said, and revealed his ace high flush.

"Je-sus!" Healy said, closing his eyes. "What the hell did you have?" he said to Ross.

"You paid to see Adams' cards," Ross said, gathering all the cards together, "not mine."

Clint raked in his chips as Ross passed the cards to Black.

"I could go for a break," Ross said. "What about the rest of you?"

"Why not?" Clint said, and the others agreed.

"Back in a half hour?" Ross said, and no one objected.

As they all got up from the table, Ross worked his way around to Clint and said, "Buy you a drink?"

"Sure," Clint said, "why not? You're the big winner."

"You're not doing so bad yourself," Ross said as they left the back room and headed for the bar.

TWO

"Seems to me," Thomas Ross said, "that I've heard your name somewhere before."

"Do me a favor," Clint said.

"What?"

"Don't tell me where."

"I can't remember where," Ross said, "but I will—"

"Well, when you do, keep it to yourself, huh?"

"Sure," Ross said, shrugging, "Been in San Francisco long?"

"A week."

"How'd you end up getting invited to the game?"

"Fella named Benny Paul invited me. You know him?"

"Sure," Ross said. "Benny's my talent scout."

"Talent scout?"

"Sure. He keeps his eyes open for new talent to bring into the game."

"Is the game yours?"

"The game," Ross said, "and this place."

No wonder they'd gotten such quick waiter service when they'd sat down. Ross had led Clint to the dining room rather than the bar, and a waiter had appeared almost magically.

"I see."

"If you're going to be around for a while I'd like to invite you to continue to sit in."

"How long does the game go on?"

"As long as there's someone willing to play. Players come and go, but there are always players."

Clint sized Ross up. He was in his forties, tall and barrel-chested, smooth and sure of himself.

"How'd you come to own this place?" Clint asked.

Ross grinned and said, "I won it."

"I had a feeling you'd say that."

"How else would a gambler like me own a place like this, in Portsmouth Square?" Ross asked. "Most of these hotels and casinos are owned by people who don't gamble. They're the smart ones."

"You seem to do pretty well."

"You can go cold just as quickly as you get hot," Ross said. "I'm sure you know that."

"Oh, I know it, all right. I was running pretty cold until I got here."

"Well, as long as you're hot, why not keep playing in the game?"

"Wouldn't you rather have someone whose luck is cold sit in?"

Ross shook his head.

"No, I like the competition. I like the way you play, Clint. You're a challenge."

"And the others?"

"They're all competent, except maybe for Healy, but then he's got the money to play the way he does."

"Are they all locals?"

"All of the men in the game right now are, but that could change very quickly."

Ross checked his watch and said. "The half hour's nearly up. Coming back?"

"For a while. While the night is young, anyway."

"What happens when the the night gets older?" Ross asked as they stood up, preparing to leave.

"There are other forms of recreation," Clint said.

"Oh, I see," Ross said, knowingly. "I think you and I have a lot in common, Clint."

Clint didn't comment on that. He was still wondering what would happen when Ross remembered where he knew him from. When it finally happened—and depending on Ross's reaction—he might have to find someplace else to gamble than the Golden Ace.

Clint Adams had been in San Francisco four days when he met Delinda Griffin.

He was playing roulette at the Alhambra—just passing the time, since he hated the game—when she walked in. She drew

9

the eye of every sane man in the room, and probably the women, as well. The men's looks were of admiration, while the women undoubtedly saw her as a threat.

She was a tall, full-bodied woman in her early thirties, with long black hair and a creamy complexion. She dressed in black, and the effect was startling and erotic. She wore very little makeup, but what there was had been expertly applied. She had real eyebrows, not the plucked variety that a lot of women had begun to wear, and she had a real nose, not one of the "pug" or "cute" varieties. In point of fact, it was her slightly large nose that kept her from being a classic beauty. Had she a more refined nose she might have been more beautiful, but she could not have been more attractive or desirable than she was at that very moment.

Clint watched her, as did all the other men, as she walked across the floor to the blackjack table. Clint played his number one more time—and hit—and then took his winnings to the blackjack table, where he sat beside her.

Later that night, she went to his room with him, where they made love. She stayed until morning, when they had breakfast.

When he was finished playing poker tonight, she'd be waiting for him in his room.

Poker and a woman like Delinda, that's what he had come to San Francisco for.

He'd end up getting a lot more than that.

THREE

Clint played for a couple of more hours and left the game a thousand dollars ahead. There were scowls from some of the other players, who thought he might be leaving the table with their money for good, but he promised all that he would return again.

When he returned to his room he found Delinda waiting, as he'd expected, only she was asleep in his bed. He undressed and slid in next to her.

Delinda moaned in her sleep now and turned over. He pulled the sheet down so that her breasts were exposed, and then propped himself on his elbow to admire them. They were large and firm, and—sadly—would probably begin to sag from their own weight as she grew older. Her scent was a warm mixture of perfume and her own earthy smell, which he liked very much. He inhaled her now, and his penis grew rigid.

She had pale nipples that were extremely sensitive. At one point the previous night, while she had ridden him, he had pressed her breasts together and sucked both nipples at one time. She had reacted with an immediate orgasm. He leaned over now and ran his tongue over the right nipple, and it immediately tightened, becoming harder. He did the same to the left and he could tell by her breathing that she was awake.

He ran his tongue down the space between her breasts, tasting her salt, burrowed his nose into the hair beneath her arms, inhaling her heady scent, then continued on down over her navel, nipped at her rust-colored pubic hair and then slid along her slick, fragrant mound.

When he found her clit and flicked at it she came awake abruptly, sucked air in between her teeth saying, "Je-sus!" and reached for his head to hold it there. He continued to lick her until she became gushingly moist, and then he started to lap at her like a thirsty dog. She closed her rounded, heavy thighs on him, as if to trap him there.

Reaching beneath her, he cupped her smooth, plump ass in his large hands and lifted her off the bed so he could thrust his tongue deeply inside her. She gasped and began to babble too fast for him to understand what she was saying, and that excited him even more.

He brought her to a shattering climax, then slid up onto her, poking at her wet opening with the spongy head of his penis. He slid into her just so much—just enough to get the head wet—and then out again. This time when she spoke he was able to make out a curse word or two.

"Jesus Christ, Clint" she said breathlessly. "Dammit, don't you dare tease me. Put it in, please!"

With that she grabbed for his butt, sank her nails into his flesh, and he in turn sank into her to the hilt.

"Oh, yeah!" she moaned.

"Yesss!" he said.

He continued to plunge in and out of her, and she fought to match the tempo of his hips with her own. Once she found the right rhythm they simply went on slamming into each other, the sound of moist flesh slapping moist flesh filling the room, mixed with their harsh breathing and squeaking of the cheap bed springs. She was so wet that his penis made loud sucking sounds as he pulled out of her and drove back in.

Then he found her mouth with his and kissed her. She opened her mouth immediately, her tongue searching for his. She moaned into his mouth, scraped her nails across his back, and shifted her legs. He knew that she was approaching orgasm.

Because they had spent several nights together already he knew what to expect when she came, she went crazy, moaning and bucking beneath him like some wild, untamed mare, and he stayed with her, riding her until his own climax spilled out like a flash flood . . .

Later she slid down between his legs and began to lick his penis which, flaccid, was still larger than most that she had seen. She cupped his balls, fondling them, and worked on him, sucking wetly, licking, even biting, until his huge organ was pulsing and ready, and then she went at him eagerly. She sucked him and fondled him until he was on the brink, then did something to him to keep him from climaxing. From there she'd start in on him again, her well-educated mouth and hands teasing him, letting him think that he was about to come, then stopping him and starting over again.

Convulsively he reached for her head, holding it tightly, his legs weak and shaky, and she finally allowed him to ejaculate.

Clint woke first in the morning. He was ravenously hungry. He'd found that to be the case each morning after he'd spent the night with Delinda. She was still asleep, snoring gently. As hungry as he was for food, he found his penis thickening as he looked down at her sleeping form.

He reached down between her thighs and delved into her with his middle finger. She moaned and squirmed, turning instantly wet, and when he slid a second finger into her moist depths, she turned over and opened herself up to him, still partly asleep.

Clint slid down between her thighs and drank from her, trying his best to bury his face inside of her. She moaned aloud, lifted her hips, and pressed against his face as his tongue entered her. He then moved atop her and slid the head of his penis into her. She was steamy hot, and although he'd intended to tease her, he found himself unable to do anything but raise himself over her and sink to the hilt inside of her.

"Oooh, yes," she moaned, wrapping her arms and legs around him. He continued to slam in and out of her until, with a great groan, he emptied himself into her in what he was sure were gallon spurts. . . .

"I think I died that time," she said, lying on her back with her arms and legs spread out.

"Does that mean you don't want breakfast?" he asked. He was on his feet, getting dressed.

"Bite your tongue," she said, rolling over in preparation of rising. She looked at him over her shoulder and asked. "What is it about sex with you that makes a gal so hungry, Clint Adams?"

"Funny," he said, "I was thinking the same thing about you. . . . "

FOUR

Jack Forster answered the door of his hotel room and saw that there were two women standing in the hall outside. His bellman had outdone himself this time.

"Ladies, please," he said, standing aside. "Enter."

The girls stepped past him and he closed the door behind thim.

"I see you've been expecting us ," one girl said.

"How could you tell?" he asked.

"It helps that you're naked," the second girl said.

He grinned and said, "Smart girls."

"Where are you from?" the first girl asked, undressing.

"Australia."

"Where's that?" the other one asked, also shedding her clothes while Jack watched with pleasure. His penis was growing larger with each passing second.

"Far away, across the sea."

Both girls' eyes widened as his penis continued to swell, and the first one asked, "Are all men from Australia as big as you?"

"Ladies," he said proudly, "believe me when I tell you that you have got the pick of the litter."

He'd requested full-bodied women, and he wasn't disappointed. Both women were young and fleshy—almost fat—with large breasts and buttocks, rounded bellies, and full thighs. They both smelled fresh and clean. When they had all of their clothes off they "oohed" and "aahed" and ran their hands over his hard chest and muscles. One girl got behind him and, putting her hands on his buttocks, pushed him. The other girl boldly took hold of his penis with one hand and pulled. In this way they led him to the freestanding bathtub in a corner of the room. The room with a bath had cost him plenty, but that was okay. He'd be rolling in money soon enough.

When he was in the water they scrubbed him down with soap, one doing his back and the other his front. As one woman leaned over the tub to scrub his penis and balls, he reached up and palmed one of her heavy breasts. The nipple was large and hard, poking at the center of his palm as he hefted the weight of the breast. The girl smiled at him, but otherwise did not respond, simply continued to scrub him. She stroked his penis with a wash cloth, doing a particularly good job of cleaning him, and then did the same to his balls. By the time she finished, his penis was red and aching.

The girl behind him slid her hands beneath his buttocks at one point, and he lifted himself so that she could clean his bottom.

When they were done they assisted him out of the tub and began to dry him with towels. The first girl dried his buttocks, back, and shoulders while the second girl dried his chest and belly, the insides of his thighs, and his penis and balls. She squeezed his penis and when a small drop of semen, like a pearl, oozed out of the tip, she licked it away.

The girls exchanged a look and nodded to each other. He was about to ask what was going on, when the girl in front of him opened her mouth and drew the spongy, bulbous head of his penis into it, fondling his testicles at the same time.

"Jesus," he said as he watched her take more and more of him into her mouth, her plump cheeks bulging. At one point he thought he felt himself bump into the back of her throat, but she made some sort of adjustment and took more of him. From behind him he could feel the mouth of the second girl peppering him with kisses, but it was the first girl who had most of his attention. Finally, she began to bob her head back and forth, sucking him wetly. She held the base of his penis while the other girl slid her head between his thighs and began to lick his balls. He felt the rush building in his legs. When he started to ejaculate it was all he could do to keep from shouting. . . .

"Christ . . . " he said, breathing heavily.

"You're paying for all night, right?" the first girl asked.

"Sure," he said, "but I need a few minutes. . . ."

The first girl licked his flaccid penis and, smiling, said, "We'll take care of that."

From behind him the second girl suddenly put a hand on each of his buttocks and, spreading them, probed his anus with her tongue until his penis rose to full mast. The girl in front, who had already sucked him once, bent her head to the task again.

She gobbled his penis, taking as much as she could into her mouth, and the girl behind him was working her mouth downward, now, between his legs until she was licking his balls again. For a moment he wondered if the girls knew any other way of doing things when the second girl moved her head . He felt a momentary sense of loss, but it was short lived as she moved around in from of him.

Both girls were licking him now, and the second girl took him in her mouth as deeply as the first one had, while the first continued to lick that portion of his penis which was still exposed.

When he was almost ready to come they both moved their mouths.

"What—" he began.

"The bed," one of them said, breathlessly.

Willingly, he laid down on the bed and the second girl immediately swallowed his penis again. The first girl supported her weight on her hands and feet and hovered above his face, just brushing him with her womanhood. He flicked his tongue out and tasted her, and when she felt his tongue she came down on his face, still holding most of her weight on her hands and knees.

He sucked the girl enthusiastically and moved his hips in unison with the other girl's sucking. Again, when he was ready the girl abandoned him, but only momentarily. When she returned it was to swallow him into her womanhood, bringing all of her weight down on his hips.

The second girl now bounced up and down on the length of his shaft while the first continued to grind her deliciously fragrant and wet womanhood into his face. Jack put his hands on her buttocks and supported her weight, because as she approached climax she could no longer support herself. Holding her that way he was able to reach deeper inside of her with his tongue, and felt her begin to tremble just as his own climax was building.

The three of them did not come together, but it was close enough so that their cries intermingled, making him wonder if anyone outside the room—or the hotel for that matter—could hear them. . . .

In the morning, after the girls left, he realized that he had never even gotten their names.

He also realized that it didn't mean diddly, because he'd never see them again. In two days time he'd be on a ship back to Australia, and he'd really only been able to financially afford one night like this one.

For all he knew, he might have only *physically* been able to survive one night like this one, too. The last thing he needed was to die of a heart attack before he could get back home and put his plan into effect, the plan which would make him the richest man in Australia.

FIVE

Clint woke early the next morning, as had been his habit since arriving in San Francisco. He slipped out of bed without awaking Delinda, dressed, and left the room. In Clint's opinion an early breakfast was something to be savored, but Delinda did not share his feelings. In fact, from what Clint knew of her she rarely ate breakfast and ate very little dinner. He wondered if she made up for it at lunch, but not having shared that meal with her, he didn't know.

He went down to the empty hotel dining room and was shown to a table. The waiter, knowing Clint's routine by now, immediately brought him a pot of strong, black coffee. Clint enjoyed eating this early in the large, empty dining room, knowing that everyone else was sleeping late after gambling and drinking and doing whatever else they did the night before.

There was one other man in the room, though, a large gent who was looking somewhat hungover himself. On one of the chairs at his table was a large hat with a wide band, the brim of which was pushed up on one side. Clint had seen hats with the brim pushed up in the front, but never on the side.

The man looked up abruptly, as if he'd sensed that he was being watched, and Clint raised his cup to him. The man hesitated, then responded in kind. Clint didn't recall having seen the man in the hotel before, but that didn't matter. Even if the fellow had been there a week, there was no reason their paths would have crossed.

The waiter came back into the dining room carrying not only Clint's breakfast, but the other man's as well. He served the other man his food, then brought Clint's plate to his table.

"There you go, Mr. Adams," the man said. "Eggs, potatoes, ham, medium rare steak, and biscuits—did I forget anything?"

"Nothing, Art. Thanks."

"My pleasure, sir. Signal if you need anything else."

"I sure will."

Clint was about to start on his breakfast when a man stepped into the doorway of the dining room, spotted him, and came over to his table.

"You looking for me?" Clint asked Luke Short.

"How'd you guess," Short said, sitting down. Short was dapper, not a large man, but competent-looking—which he was. He had a carefully tended mustache and a .38 hidden away in a shoulder rig. He was as deadly with the gun as he was with a deck of cards.

"Coffee?"

"Sure."

The waiter had brought two cups—in case, Clint supposed, Delinda decided to join him—and Clint filled one for Short.

"I checked in last night and heard you were here."

"Heard from who?" Clint asked.

"Thomas Ross."

"You know Ross well?" Clint asked.

"We're acquainted," Short said. "We've spent some time at the same poker table."

"Are you here for his game?"

"I am."

"Want some breakfast?"

"I'll steal a biscuit and a slice of ham," Short said, reaching across the table and doing so.

"Help yourself," Clint said, because Short already had.

Short broke the biscuit in half and slid the ham between the two pieces.

"You playing?" Short asked.

"I did last night."

"How did you do?"

"Came out a bit ahead."

"Playing tonight?"

"I was planning on it."

"Was?"

"Now that I know you're playing, I might just save my money."

"Bullshit," Short said. "You're every bit as good a player as I am—when you put your mind to it."

25

"That's kind of you to say—"

"You let your mind wander too much," Short continued. "If you ever did it just for the money you'd drive me away from the table, but you do it too much for fun."

"I enjoy it."

"I hate it."

"Why do you play, then?" Clint asked.

"Because I'm good at it."

Short tucked the last piece of biscuit and ham into his mouth, chewed it thoughtfully, and then washed it down with the remainder of his coffee.

"More coffee?"

Short held up his hand.

"I have to go and buy a suit."

"One of those special suits?"

Short was known to wear suits with a holster already sewn into it, so that he wouldn't have to wear a shoulder rig.

"One of those suits," Short said, nodding and rising. "See you tonight?"

"I'll sit in for a while."

"Good. Enjoy your breakfast."

"I intend to," Clint said, and Short left.

Clint applied himself to doing just that until he got the feeling someone was watching him. He looked up and caught the other man in the room looking at him. The man raised his coffee cup in greeting, and Clint did the same. At that point the man rose, and Clint saw that he was indeed a large man, six feet four or five, at least. The waiter came over so the man could pay his bill, and then the big man picked up his funny-looking hat and left.

"Can I get you anything, Mr. Adams?" the waiter came over and asked.

"Another pot of coffee, Art."

"Sure."

"Art, who was that fella?"

"That was Mr. Forster, sir," the waiter said.

"A guest in the hotel?"

"Yes sir."

"For how long?"

"At least as long as you, sir."

"Where's he from?"

"Australia."

"Australia? What's he doing here?"

"I don't know what he's doing here, Mr. Adams, but I do know that he's heading back to Australia in a mattter of days."

"Interesting. Forster, you said?"

"Yes, sir. Forster, Jack Forster. I'll get that coffee."

"Thanks."

For a moment Clint wondered what it was like in Australia, then turned his attention back to his plate, before the remainder of his breakfast went cold.

SIX

Outside on the street, Jack Forster paused to light a cigar and think about the man he'd seen in the dining room. According to the waiter the fella was somebody called the Gunsmith, real name: Clint Adams. In the short time Jack had been in this country he'd never been out of California, so the name was not familiar to him. Again, though, according to the waiter, this man was one of the legends of the West, one of those magical gunmen they wrote books about.

If Jack was going to be in this country longer than another couple of days, it might have been interesting to make the acquaintance of such a man.

He shook his head and wondered if he'd ever regret forgoing the opportunity to meet a real living legend.

Clint was just finishing his second pot of coffee when another man stepped into the dining room. By this time there were other diners present, although the room was still more empty than full. The man in the doorway swept the room with his eyes, saw Clint, and walked over.

"Lieutenant Manson, isn't it?" Clint asked.

"That's right," the well-dressed man said.

Harry Manson was a lieutenant on the San Francisco Police Department, and his bailiwick was Portsmouth Square. He endeared himself to the hotel and gambling house owners and, for all Clint knew, also endeared himself to their money.

On Clint's first night in town he'd been approached by the lieutenant, briefly questioned, and politely warned. It seemed the lieutenant was aware of his reputation and had promised to keep an eye on him.

"Keeping your promise, I see," Clint said.

"Promise? Oh, that," Manson said. "To tell you the truth, I'm quite impressed. You've been here almost a week and haven't been in trouble."

"I told you that first day, Lieutenant," Clint said, "I don't like trouble."

"Well, unfortunately, all I had to evaluate you on was your reputation."

"And now?"

"Now I'm not as concerned."

"I'm glad to hear it."

The lieutenant stood silently for a few moments, perhaps waiting for an invitation to sit. He wouldn't get one from Clint, who didn't like the man. Manson was in his early thirties and obviously thought much of himself. He appeared competent enough, a solid six-footer with heavy sideburns adorning his strong features, but he had not made a good impression on Clint that first night, and nothing was happening now to make Clint change his mind.

"Well, I'll be going, then," Manson said. "I just thought I'd, uh, check up on you and see how you're doing."

"I'm doing just fine."

"How are the tables treating you?"

"I'm doing just fine," Clint repeated.

"Ah, well, then, good morning."

"Good morning, Lieutenant."

As the policeman left, Clint signaled for the waiter. As he did so, he noticed a look of distaste of the man's face.

"Who is that look for?" Clint asked. "A bad customer?"

"A bad policeman," Art said.

"Manson?"

"The same."

"What makes him bad?"

"I've wondered that myself," Art said, and then realized how Clint meant the question. "He's lining his pockets with money that ain't rightly his—but maybe I shouldn't be saying." Suddenly, the waiter looked frightened, as if perhaps he'd said too much.

"You don't have to be afraid to say what you think to me, Art," Clint said. He rose, paid the man, and tipped him generously.

"Thanks, Mr. Adams."

"That's all right, Art. Thanks for giving me your opinions."

"Uh, sure . . . but I wouldn't want Mr. Thomas to find out—"

"Don't worry, Art," Clint said, patting the man on the back.

"It's just between you and me."

"I appreciate it, Mr. Adams. Have a good day."

"You, too, Art," Clint said, "you, too."

Clint left the dining room and went upstairs to wake Delinda the best way he knew how.

SEVEN

That night Clint told Delinda over dinner that he was going to the Barbary Coast.

"Why, in heaven's name?" she asked.

"Just for a change."

"I thought you had a poker game to play in?"

"I do," he said. "I'll be back for it."

"I hope so," she said. "I've heard terrible stories about the Barbary Coast."

"Well," he said, rising, and moving around to hold her chair while she did the same, "later tonight I'll tell you if all the stories are true or not."

Jack Forster decided that he'd rather spend his time—and money—down on the Coast than in the fancy casinos of Portsmouth Square.

He could use a little excitement before he left America.

Jack Forster got to the Blood Bucket before Clint Adams did.

When Clint entered the Blood Bucket he wondered why he had come. Had he already grown tired of the fancy-dressed gamblers in Portsmouth Square? Wasn't there anyplace he could go and truly relax and feel comfortable?

He doubted it.

He walked to the bar, found a slim space, and wedged himself into it. He drew a dirty look from the men on either side of him, but they grudgingly moved to accommodate him.

He ordered a beer, and frosty mug in hand, turned to look the room over. Almost immediately he saw the big man he'd seen at breakfast—Jack Forster, wasn't that it?—sitting at a table playing poker with four other men. He pushed away from the bar and moved into a position from where he could watch the game, but he could not hear what was being said.

There was a hand of five-card stud going on, and although he couldn't see everyone's cards he could see Jack Forster's. He had four hearts in front of him, and was betting them.

There was only one player still in the game with him, and when that man folded his cards, the big man flipped over his hole card, even though no one had paid to see it.

It was black.

Clint saw the look on the other man's face, and then saw another look pass between him and the man across from him.

He edged closer to the table.

The deal went to the man on Jack Forster's right. The glance had been exchanged by the man across from him, and the man on his left.

"I'll open for five," Jack Forster said.

Everybody called and then took their cards. Forster took two.

Suddenly, the game changed.

The man on Jack Forster's right began to raise, and from Clint's vantage point he could not see the man's cards.

He had nothing.

He had the kind of hand where it would be ridiculous to even try and bluff.

Across the table from Jack Forster the man was also raising.

Everyone else dropped out until it was Jack Forster and the two men who Clint had decided were working together. He didn't know if they had been all through the game, but they were now.

When the play came back to Jack Forster the Australian said, "Well, I'll just see the two raises and raise twenty dollars myself."

"You must have a good hand," the man on his left said.

"It's good enough," the big man said.

It's better than yours, Clint thought. He debated the wisdom of saying something. He wasn't involved in the game and by all rights should mind his own business, but he hated cheaters. Stepping in would be looking for trouble, and he wasn't supposed to be in San Francisco for that.

Off to his right he noticed that there were two other men who were a little more interested in the game than they should be. He wondered if they had a friend in the game— or maybe two?

"I'll call," the man on Jack Forster's left said.

"Well, I could raise again," the other man said, "but I think it's time to call a stop to this and get on to the next hand, so I'll just call."

"I've got three kings," Jack Forster said.

"Beats me," the man on his left said.

At that point Clint saw the man put his right hand in his jacket pocket, and he moved closer to the table until he was standing directly behind him.

"What have you got?" Forster asked the man across the table from him.

That man put his cards down, but did not spread them.

"I've got a flush."

"I guess you win, then," Forster said, "but let's see the cards."

"Yeah," the man on his left said, "spread them out," and began to reach across the table for them.

Clint was about to move forward and jostle the man's chair when a huge knife suddenly appeared in the Australian's left hand, the sharp point pressed against the man's temple.

Suddenly, all attention was on that table, and the place grew quiet.

Death hung heavy right over the table, and everyone was waiting to see where it would fall.

EIGHT

"Now," Forster said, "let me make this very clear, so there won't be any mistakes. I'm calling the hand that's on the table, not the one in your hand."

"What are you talking—" the man began, but the Australian reached out with his other hand and closed it around the man's wrist. He applied pressure and the man gasped, dropping the cards he'd palmed to the table.

"*That* hand is a flush," Jack Forster said, "but what's this one?" Using his right hand he spread the cards that were on the table. "Three hearts, a club and a spade," he said. "That don't look like a flush to me. You fellas been cheating all night, or just since I sat down?"

There was no answer.

"What about it?" he asked the other two men at the table. "Have they been spreading each other's cards?"

"A couple of times, yeah," one of them said, as if it had just dawned on him.

"All right friends," Forster said, "stand up and leave quietly."

The man across from him reached for his chips and Forster increased the pressure on his knife.

"Jesus!" said the man with the knife to his head, and the other man froze.

"Leave the money."

"That's my money!" the man across the table snapped.

"Leave it!"

"Jesus Christ, Will, leave it!" the man next to Forster cried out.

Clint watched the half-standing man, to see if he'd go for his gun. Instead he looked away from the table, at the two men Clint noticed earlier. Clint looked at them and saw them start for their guns.

"I wouldn't do that!" he called out.

The two men froze, and the big Australian looked at Clint with a sideward glance.

"These two have two friends behind you," Clint told him. "I doubt their intentions are too honorable as far as you're concerned."

"Can you handle them?" Forster asked.

"If need be," Clint said. "You just worry about your two."

Forster nodded and turned his attention back to the two

men. The other two men studied Clint, wondering if they should try him.

"All right, gentlemen," Forster said, "now get up easy and leave—without the money."

"You won't get away with this," the man across the table said.

"Yes, I will. It wouldn't be wise for you to try me, friend."

They stared at each other for a few moments, and then the man called Will backed away from the table.

"You got a knife and I got a gun."

"But my knife is against this man's head."

"That's his lookout."

"Will, Jesus!"

"Shut up! I ain't leavin' without my money!"

Clint watched the tableau from the corner of his eye, very interested in seeing how the big Australian would handle the situation.

"Go ahead," the big man said, "pull your gun."

And the man did.

He drew, and as he did, Jack Forster rose and pulled the other man in front of him. The table went flying, as did the other two players, and then the man with the gun fired.

The shot struck the man Forster was holding, and then Forster propelled the man foward, smack into the man with the gun. Both men went tumbling to the floor, and before anybody could move the Australian was there. He reached down and took hold of the wrist of the man holding the gun. He pulled him to his feet, raised the arm over his head, and squeezed until the gun dropped from the man's nervous fingers.

"Jesus," he cried, "you're breaking my wrist!"

"Not yet," Jack Forster said, and then he increased the

pressure until everyone heard the bones snap. "Now it's broken," he said, and released the man's wrist.

"Aw, Christ!" the man cried out in pain, falling to the floor, cradling his injured arm. The other man, who'd been shot by his own "friend," had not moved.

Forster turned then and looked at Clint.

"What about his friends?"

Clint inclined his head toward the two men in question and said, "Drop your gunbelts, boys. We'll be having a visit from the law, soon."

Forster looked over at the two men.

"We didn't do nothing," one of them said.

"Tell it to the law," Clint said. "Drop them or use them."

They made the wise choice, unbuckled their belts, and dropped them.

"I'm in your debt, friend," Jack Forster said. Then he frowned and said, "Don't I know you?"

"We had breakfast together today," Clint said, and then added, "sort of."

NINE

After they had cleared everything up with the law, Clint and Jack went back to their hotel in Portsmouth Square, where Jack insisted on buying Clint a drink.

Over the drink Jack said, "You don't find that kind of excitement here in the Square much, do you?"

"It's here," Clint said, "it's just not so much out in the open—and here, it's over a lot more money."

"I'll bet," Jack said. "You ever play in any of those high-stakes games?"

"Sometimes. You?"

"Never. In fact, I never even played until I came to this country six months ago."

"You've only been playing six months and you spotted those cheaters?" Clint asked. "I'm impressed."

"Don't be. I'm a fast learner."

"What brought you to this country, Jack?"

"What else? Gold"

"Find any?"

"Some, not much, but—"

"But what?"

Jack studied Clint for a moment, then nodded to himself, as if he'd made a decision.

"You backed me tonight and you didn't even know me, Clint," Jack said. "That makes you trustworthy in my book."

"Well, I hope so."

Jack leaned his elbows on the table and lowered his voice.

"I think there's gold in Australia, Clint."

"What makes you say that?"

"The land. I've been working here—the land here in California resembles the land in my home of Bathurst, in New South Wales. I mean, if I let myself, I can believe I'm in Australia."

"And that's why you're going back home?"

"Well, I'm going back because I miss it," Jack said, "but I wouldn't be making the trip if I didn't think there was gold to be found."

"Well, I hope you're right, Jack."

"I've got an idea," Jack said, suddenly.

"What?"

"Why don't you come with me?"

"Me? Go to Australia?"

"Sure, why not? There'll be plenty of gold. We could be partners."

"You don't owe me that much, Jack—"

"That's bull. I probably owe you my life, but I like you, as well. I'd like you to be my partner."

"Australia . . ." Clint said. He didn't know anything about the country, but by the same token, neither did it know anything about him.

That made it tempting.

"Why don't you think about it?" Jack suggested.

"I will, Jack," Clint said. He emptied his beer mug and set it down on the table. "I'll give it a lot of thought tonight."

"Good. The ship leaves day after tomorrow, and I'm sure we can get you passage, as well. It's nothing fancy, and we might even have to do a little work."

"A little work never bothered me."

"Good, good."

"I've got an appointment, Jack," Clint said.

"One of those big games?"

"Yes, but before I go, tell me a little about Australia."

"Telling you isn't going to make it sound pretty."

He explained how for a long time all Australia was a penal colony, inhabited and worked by the dregs of humanity, the worst criminals the world could supply. Now, though, they had cities and ranches. The land was growing, and when Jack found the gold he knew was there, he was hoping to use it to help Australia grow even more.

"For instance," he said, "if I had enough money, I'd bring stagecoaches to Australia for transportation over the long distances between settlements and cities. And the riverboats that we have, I'd use them to supply gambling. Australians love to gamble, Clint, especially on horse racing. If we had a fast horse, we could make money."

For a moment Clint thought about Duke, who was now in the hotel livery.

"If you don't have stagecoaches there now you could make a fortune just doing that."

"But I need the money to start it off. That's where the gold will come in. When I have enough money I'll be able to bring the best stagecoach in America to Australia."

"That would be the Concord coach."

"See!" Jack said, excitedly. "We'd make fine partners! Come on Clint. Do it!"

Clint laughed.

"Like I said, Jack," he said, rising. "I'll have to give it some thought. I'll see you tomorrow."

As Clint started to walk away, Jack called out his name.

"Yeah?" Clint replied.

"I understand you're something of a—well, a legend here in America," Jack said. "Would that be a reason you might not want to leave?"

"No, Jack," Clint said, truthfully, "that would be the reason that I *would*."

TEN

When Clint got to the game it was late, and he didn't think he'd even get two hours of play in. From the looks of things, Luke Short was winning big, Thomas Ross was holding his own, and everyone else was losing. Everyone who had been there the night before was there again, except for Healy. His chair was empty, and Clint took it.

Short looked at Clint in surprise and said, "I didn't think you were coming."

"Something came up. My deal?"

"The cards are yours," Thomas Ross said. "Let's see what you can do with them."

When Clint went back to his room that night—or very early that morning—he had lost five hundred of the thousand dollars that he had won the night before. That was all right, though, because he knew why. He hadn't really been concentrating on the cards, something that Luke Short had obviously noticed.

After the game was called for the night, Short went over to Clint and said, "Where was your mind tonight, boy?"

"Australia."

"What?" Short asked, puzzled.

"Never mind, Luke," Clint said, "never mind. I'll see you tomorrow."

When he entered the room he saw that Delinda wasn't there. She had probably awakened and, seeing how late it was, given up on him and gone to her own room. Briefly he considered following her there but decided against it.

He had some thinking to do.

ELEVEN

In the morning Clint found Jack having breakfast and joined him.

"Why hadn't I seen you here before yesterday?" Clint asked after ordering breakfast.

"Up till yesterday I was rising late. I guess I'm practicing so I'll make my ship tomorrow."

"It's leaving early?"

"Fairly early," Jack said. "Nine A.M."

"When is it getting in?"

"Today." Jack leaned forward and said, "Ever been on an overseas voyage, Clint?"

"No. I've never been on anything bigger than a riverboat, and then only for a matter of days."

"This would be a matter of days," Jack said, with a smile, "forty, maybe fifty, depending on the winds and the water."

"Forty days at sea?" Clint asked.

"You're not afraid of getting seasick, are you?"

"No . . . of course not."

"Good," Jack said. "It's good that you're not afraid of it. You will get sick, of course, but it's good that you're not afraid."

"Thanks a lot."

They paused while Clint's breakfast was served, and then Jack leaned foward.

"You're coming, aren't you?"

"I don't know," Clint said evasively.

"Maybe you'd better take a look at the boat, huh?" Jack suggested.

"Maybe that'd be a good idea."

"We can take a walk to the dock later and see if it's in. I can also talk to my contact there."

"Contact?"

"Yes, the man who got me passage even though it's not a passenger vessel. By working, I get a cheap price—and you will too."

"I wouldn't know what to do on a boat."

"You'd just have to follow my lead," Jack said. "I did it on the way over."

"There's one other problem," Clint said.

"What's that?"

"My horse."

"Where is it?"

48

"In the livery."

"Sell it; we've got horses in Australia."

Clint looked at Jack in shock.

"I can't sell Duke."

"You have a name for your horse?"

"He has a name, yes."

"Is he a racehorse?"

"No."

"The only horses I ever knew that were named were racing animals." Jack frowned and said, "I don't think I understand."

Clint stared at Jack, then said, "After breakfast I'll take you to meet him. Then you'll understand."

"Now I understand," Jack said as soon as he laid eyes on Duke.

Clint walked into the stall with the big black gelding and stroked his massive neck.

"How you doing, big boy?"

Duke bobbed his head up and down.

"Jesus," Jack said. "He looks like that *and* he understands you?"

"Now you see why I'd never consider selling him," Clint said.

"I see. He's worth a fortune."

"He's not mine to sell," Clint said.

"Whose is he, then?"

"He doesn't belong to anyone."

"You mean if he wanted to go his own way, you'd let him?" Jack asked in disbelief.

"Of course."

"But he doesn't, right?"

"Not so far."

Jack moved in for a closer look.

"Is he fast?"

"Yes, and he can run all day."

"That's even better," Jack said. "Clint, if we race him in Australia, we'll make a fortune. Would you be willing to race him?"

"If he wants to run," Clint said, "I'll let him."

"You'd have to ride him, though, right?"

"Of course."

"He'd go faster with a lighter man on his back."

Clint stroked Duke's sleek neck one more time, then stepped out of the stall.

"He won't let anyone else ride him."

"No," Jack said, "I guess he wouldn't. Jesus, I hope we can get him on the boat."

"If he doesn't go, I don't," Clint said.

Jack's face split into a huge grin.

"You're going, then?"

Clint realized with a start that he had decided to do just that.

"Yeah, I'm going."

Maybe, Clint thought as they left the livery, maybe where nobody knew him, he'd be able to relax.

Finally.

TWELVE

Just before lunch time they went down to the San Francisco docks to see if the boat had arrived.

"One thing," Jack said.

"What?"

"While we're aboard, don't refer to it as a boat. They like to call them ships."

"Same thing, isn't it?"

"Just say 'boat' when we're on board and you'll find out."

"That's if I get on board," Clint said.

"There she is."

Clint looked at the boat. He didn't know whether to be

impressed or not. He didn't know anything about boats—or ships. It was certainly larger than anything he'd ever seen, and there were what looked like poles sticking up from the deck. He assumed that each pole would hold a sail.

He'd seen pictures.

"What do you think?"

Clint shrugged.

"Let me see if I can find my man," Jack said. "Why don't you look around."

"Okay," Clint said, "I'll look around."

Clint walked along the docks, eyeing the different boats—ships. He wondered if he should be suspicious of Jack Forster, who wanted him to go to Australia so badly. Did he just want a partner, or was there some other reason?

What other reasons could there be?

Maybe that was just another reason he *should* go to Australia. Here in America he *had* to be suspicious of anyone who spoke to him or looked at him; he had to wonder if they knew who he was.

In Australia, nobody would know who he was. He could start clean.

He walked back to where the boat they would sail on was docked and looked it over. It looked sturdy enough.

He wondered idly if he *would* get sick out on the open sea. If he didn't, maybe he'd discard his guns and become a sailor.

Ah, if he did that, what would happen to Duke?

Maybe he'd just go to Australia for a little rest.

Hell of a long way to go for some rest. . . .

"Hey, Clint!"

He turned and saw Jack Forster bearing down on him, grinning happily.

"You been standing here the whole time?"

"I walked around a bit. Did you see your man?"

"Yes. You've got passage, if you want it."

"And Duke?"

"And Duke. . . . But it'll cost you."

"How much?"

Jack told him.

A long way to go . . . and a lot of money. . . .

They went back to the hotel for lunch and ate in relative silence. After they finished eating, Clint told Jack that he decided to go.

"Even for that much money?"

"Sure, why not?"

"I knew it," Jack said. "You won't regret it, Clint. We're going to strike it rich in Australia."

"Sure."

"Have you got it?"

"Got what?"

"The money for passage for you and the horse?"

If Clint had more time, he'd have been able to get the money from his bank in Labyrnth, Texas, but he wasn't sure if he did have the time. There'd have to be a wire sent, and then another back. . . .

"After tonight," Clint said, "I will."

"Poker?"

Clint nodded.

"Are you that good?"

"A man told me once that I could be," Clint said, "if I concentrated on the cards. I guess we're going to find out if he was right."

THIRTEEN

"I haven't seen you all day," Delinda complained.

She had been waiting for him when he got back to his room.

"I'm sorry," he said. "I've been busy."

"Doing what?"

"Planning my departure."

She raised her eyebrows.

"You're leaving San Francisco?"

He grinned and said, "I'm leaving the country."

"The country? Was it something I said?"

He laughed and said, "No, nothing."

"Where are you going?"

"Australia."

"What's in Australia?"

"Peace, I'm hoping," he said. "I guess I'll find out when I get there."

"When are you leaving?"

"Tomorrow."

"So soon?"

"The whole thing is kind of spur of the moment, Delinda. I'm really sorry."

"No, that's all right," she said. She had been sitting in his bed and now she rose. "We had some fun together, didn't we?"

"We did."

"That was all either one of us expected from the other, wasn't it?"

"Yes."

She shrugged and said, "Well, that's that, isn't it? Is there any point to us . . . meeting later tonight?"

"Ah, I think I'm going to busy tonight."

She nodded.

"Delinda—"

She held up her hand to keep him from speaking any further.

"Have a good time in Australia, Clint. I hope you find the peace you're looking for."

He watched as she left the room and wondered if he should go after her. She actually deserved better, but she was right. All he'd been after was some companionship and some fun. She might have deserved better, but he really didn't owe her anything.

He dressed for his dinner with Jack, because he wanted to hear more about Australia. After dinner, he'd go right to the game.

They were going to see a different player at the table tonight.

FOURTEEN

Luke Short was staring across the table hard at Clint Adams. Away from the table they were friends, but seated across from one another with money on the table between them, friendship went out the window.

The other players in the game had already gone out after a raise, and now it was up to Clint.

They were playing draw, so there were no cards showing. Clint had to evaluate Short's hand the same way Short had to evaluate his—from what they already knew of each other as players, and from each other's eyes.

Clint had a full house, but it was a small one, threes over queens. He would much rather have had it the other way around. He had gone into the hand with the three threes, raising the opener, and had then drawn the two queens.

Short had raised Clint's first bet and drawn two cards. On the next round, the raiser had checked to Clint, who also checked, and then when Short bet, Clint raised him. That drew everyone's eyes and forced them out. Short raised Clint, and now it was up to him to call or raise.

Short had drawn to three cards, which meant if he had drawn to three of a kind he could also have a full house—and a higher full house than Clint's. *That* wouldn't have been hard.

In the final analysis, his move was simple. There was certainly enough money on the table, and another raise was not going to force Short out. They might as well show their cards and get on to the next hand.

"I call," Clint said.

"Ace high flush," Short said, showing his cards.

Clint didn't believe it. Short had drawn to a three-card flush and filled it.

"Full house," he said, "and a small one."

"But big enough to get the job done," Thomas Ross said, "which you seem to be doing very well tonight, Clint."

"Just the run of the cards."

Lutz, seated on Clint's right, gathered up the cards for the next deal.

"I think we should take a short break," Ross said. Since it was his game, everyone complied.

"Drink?" Short asked Clint.

"Sure."

They went downstairs, but instead of going to the restaurant they went directly to the bar.

"Your concentration is a lot better tonight."

"How could you have drawn to a three-card flush? That's not like you."

Short shrugged.

"I had a feeling."

"You playing hunches in your old age?"

"You will, too, when you get to be my age."

It was all a joke, because Luke Short was barely five years older than Clint Adams, even though he appeared to be older.

"You're playing with more of a purpose tonight," Short said.

"Am I?"

If that was meant as a form of denial, Short ignored it.

"What's the reason?"

Clint swirled the beer in his mug and said, "I'm leaving in the morning."

"For where?"

"Australia."

"Where's that?"

Clint told him where it was, and how far away it was.

"Jesus Christ," Short said. "What do you want to go there for?"

"Because nobody knows me."

Short nodded, and Clint thought he saw understanding in the man's eyes.

"Sure," Short said, "I've thought about doing that. Not going to Australia, I mean, but going somewhere where people don't know me."

"But you never did it."

"No."

"Why?"

"Because it would have meant leaving this country," Short

said. "I love this country too much to ever leave it—although I do go to Mexico every so often, but that's not what we're talking about here . . . and—" he added hastily, "—I'm not insinuating that you don't love this country."

"I didn't think you were."

"How long do you plan to stay?"

"I don't know."

"How many people have you told that you're going?"

"Only you—and now that you mention it . . . " Clint said, and took something out of his pocket. It was a piece of paper with some writing on it.

"What's this?" Short said, taking it as Clint handed it to him.

"A telegraph message. Would you send it for me tomorrow afternoon?"

"Can I read it?"

"Sure."

Short did so.

"Rick Hartman, that's your friend in Texas, isn't it?" Short asked.

"Yes."

"Why are you having me tell him that you've left the country?"

"Because he'll try to talk me out of it. I don't want anyone to try and talk me out of it."

"Do you think he could?"

"He might."

Clint didn't like admitting that, because he knew the conclusion Short would come to.

Short frowned at Clint and said, "You're not sure you're doing the right thing, are you?

"No."

"But you're going to do it, anyway."

"Yes."

"Why?"

"So that I'll never have to wonder what would have happened if I hadn't."

Again, Short nodded in understanding.

"Well, if you're going to make the money you need, we'd better get back upstairs."

"Still going to play against me while I'm hot and concentrating?"

"What kind of fun would it be to play against you when you're cold?" Short asked.

This time it was Clint who nodded in understanding.

Clint met Jack Forster for breakfast the following morning.

"How did you do?" Jack asked.

Clint grinned. "When do we catch our boat"

"Ship," Jack said, returning the grin.

FIFTEEN

Sydney, New South Wales, Australia

Clint was impressed with the size of Sydney, Australia, although he didn't know why. Probably because he didn't know what to expect. It was a large city, though, and to be perfectly truthful, it would have been very easy to believe that he was still in the United States.

It was September, and yet the weather was warm. Jack explained that when it was winter in the United States it was summer in Australia. Since it was September, it was considered the beginning of spring, and the temperature was about eighty degrees.

"We're supposedly in the cooler section of Australia."

He further explained that spring would go on until November, then summer would run from December to February. In March autumn would come in, and then give way to winter from June to August.

"Of course, winter here can't compare with winter in America. Still, it gets down into the forties, sometimes."

On the ship Jack had tried to fill Clint in on what life was like in Australia. He told him that Australia was basically cut up into four colonies. Politics were split into three groups: first, the government party; second, the landowners ("Squatters," he explained, was a respectable term in Australia); and lastly, the merchants and workers in the cities.

"I don't intend to get much involved in politics," Clint replied, and the subject was dropped.

Clint and Jack waited on the dock while Duke was unloaded, and then Clint took up the reins and they walked to the nearest hotel.

"We'll stay here and get an early start in the morning," Jack said.

"To where?"

"My home in Bathurst."

"Your home?"

"I've got a ranch, and a wife," Jack said.

"You never mentioned that."

"You never asked. The ranch will come in handy, though. We can do our prospecting there, and even run Duke from there. There'll be plenty of action in the area for horse racing."

"You're the guide," Clint said. "I'm just along for the ride."

They went into the hotel and registered, and the clerk had

someone take charge of Duke.

In his room Clint dropped his gear on the bed and walked to the window. He'd traveled light, figuring to buy appropriate clothing when they arrived. The thing that really took some getting used to was going without his gun, which was in his grip, but if he was really going to live like no one knew who he was, he couldn't go around wearing the gun in a strange country. Jack said that there were some people who carried guns, but for the most part they were rifles.

"If you wear it," Jack said, "you're going to make people wonder."

So he had taken it off and tucked it away— and he felt naked.

Another thing he felt was the pain in his hands from the calluses he'd collected working on the ship. After a couple of weeks of swabbing decks and rigging sails and whatever else they'd had him doing, he had started to wonder if he'd done the right thing. Now, however, that he was here in Australia, he was sure he had.

During the entire walk from the docks to the hotel, he hadn't drawn one look that wasn't simply an innocent glance. He hadn't had to try and read anything into the expression in anyone's eyes.

He never once wondered if the person looking at him *knew* who he was.

He was feeling the freedom already.

There was a knock at his door, and since it could only have been Jack, he called out for him to come in.

"Let's get some lunch," Jack suggested, "and then I'll show you around."

"Sounds good to me," Clint said.

Jack introduced Clint to something called "carpetbagger

steak" which was beef with rock oysters.

"It's very good," Clint said. Well, at least he wouldn't starve while he was in Australia. The food seemed palatable.

After lunch Jack showed him Sydney, which was a thriving, growing city that seemed to be in the throes of change. On almost every block there was a building under construction, either being built or improved.

"Wait until we get out into the bush," Jack said. "There won't be any buildings for miles, and when there is one it'll be a shack."

"Do you live in a shack?"

"Hell, no, I built a nice house for my bride."

"How long have you been gone?"

"Uh—" Jack said, frowning as he thought, "going on eight months, now."

"What did your wife think about you leaving?"

"I told her I was going to come back rich."

"But you haven't yet."

"No, but that'll just be a matter of time."

"Will she wait?"

"She's waited this long, hasn't she?"

To Clint that remained to be seen, but he didn't remark on it.

Instead he asked, "How long have you been married?"

"Um," Jack said, thinking again, "let me see, I been gone eight months—we've been married ten months."

"You left your wife after only two months of marriage?"

"Believe me, Clint, she understood."

"This has to be one extraordinary woman."

"You'll know just how extraordinary when you meet her."

Clint couldn't wait to meet Mrs. Jack Forster.

SIXTEEN

Before dinner they split up. Jack went to buy himself a saddle horse and to get them a pack animal, and Clint went to buy the supplies they needed for the trip.

Clint had some trouble with the money—which was pounds and shillings rather than dollars and cents—but found the clerk at the store to be very helpful and honest. He appreciated that and gave the man something extra for his trouble.

They met in front of the restaurant where they were to have dinner.

"Did you get the horses?"

"I sure did, and a good deal too. Got myself a fine animal—

though he can't compare with Duke, of course."

"Not many can. I got us some coffee and canned goods for the trip. That should hold us, don't you think?"

"I don't see why not."

"I also got the Australian equivalent of beef jerky. Should I ask you what it really is?"

"You don't want to know. Come on, let's go inside and eat."

For dinner Clint had a meat pie and then for dessert something called Pavlova, which he felt was some kind of pudding.

During dinner Jack explained the route they'd take to get to Bathurst.

"It's a fairly straight run, but it is a hundred fifty miles through some pretty deserted terrain. We'll need a good pack horse, and good saddle horses—that is, I will. You've got Duke, of course, but I wanted to talk to you about him."

"What about him?"

"I don't think you should ride him to Bathurst."

"Why not?"

"Well, if we're going to race him, I think you should rent or buy another horse, so he won't have to carry you all the way."

"We haven't really settled on the fact that we are going to race him, Jack," Clint said. "And besides, I'm not going to buy a saddle horse when I have Duke. He wouldn't like it."

"He wouldn't."

"I'll ride him."

"Well, all right," Jack said, clearly unconvinced, "I won't argue with you over it."

"Good."

After dinner Jack said, "How about getting a drink?"

"Sure."

"There's a saloon down the block from our hotel," Jack

said, "although they don't always call them saloons here. They call them pubs."

"Why?"

"Why do they call them 'saloons' in America?"

"Because they are."

"All right, then, that's why they call them 'pubs' here."

Clint decided not to pursue the subject.

Jack took him to a *saloon*, and they had a few drinks while a couple of girls who worked there joined them. They were fascinated by Clint's accent, and by the fact that he came from America.

"Ooh, it must be exciting. I've heard so much about America. What part do you come from?" a girl named Enid asked. She was a tall, willowy blonde wearing a peasant blouse that threatened to expose her breasts fully at any moment.

"Clint is from the Wild West," Jack said, putting his arm around the blonde.

"The West, how wonderful" the other woman said. Her name was Mary, and she was a chubby brunette wearing a low-cut dress that clearly showed the tops of her plump white breasts.

"Is it as wild as they say?" she asked.

"Wild?" Jack asked. "Well, let me tell you . . . " and he launched into some stories that Clint was sure weren't true at all. Soon, he lost Mary's attention, and she turned to Clint while Jack continued to regale Enid with stories of the Wild West.

"You've lived there," Mary said to Clint. "What's it really like?"

"Some of it is pretty wild and untamed," Clint said. "Some

of it is just like Sydney, cities that are growing every day."

"Like New York and San Francisco?" she asked.

"Yes. How did you know that?"

"I knew another Yank once."

"Yank?"

"Yankee."

"Oh."

Clint was unaware that the term—which had originated during the Civil War—had made it this far.

"He told me about those cities."

"What did he tell you?"

"Oh, well, for one thing, he told me he was going to take me there," she said laughing.

"Obviously he didn't"

"No, he didn't," she said, "and promise me you won't say that to me."

"I promise."

"Good. How long are you going to be in Sydney?"

"Just overnight."

"Then I guess I shouldn't waste my time waiting for *you* to ask *me*."

"Ask you what?"

"To go back to your hotel with you tonight."

"Oh, well, Mary, I should tell you that I never, uh, pay—"

She laughed, and it had a nice sound to it.

"I wasn't asking you to pay for me, Clint," she said. "For heaven's sake, I work here but that doesn't make me a whore."

"I'm sorry," Clint said, "I shouldn't have—"

"Don't apologize," she said, putting her hand on his arm. "It's all right." She squeezed his arm and said, "I'm very attracted to you, and I'd like to spend the night with you. If you don't feel the same way, just say so. It'll be all right."

"I find you very attractive, too, Mary," he said.

"Then it's settled?"

He smiled and said, "It's settled."

He looked past her at Jack, who was still telling tall tales to Enid, and gave him a quick, lewd wink.

Apparently, Jack had made the same deal with Enid.

Idly, Clint wondered about Jack's wife. Jack was fine as a friend, but it was obvious that his kind was a piss-poor excuse for a husband.

What could the woman have possibly seen in him?

Was she that desperate to get married that she took whatever treatment he dished out to her?

Clint looked over at Jack, whose face was buried in Enid's neck, and suddenly he wasn't looking forward to meeting a woman who would let Jack Forster walk all over her.

SEVENTEEN

Clint's first encounter with an Austalian woman was quite pleasant and encouraging. It seemed that neither his appetite for food, nor for women, would suffer while he was in Australia.

The four of them walked back to the hotel together, and then Jack went to Enid's room while Clint took Mary to his. Inside, Mary wasted no time in disrobing and giving him his first look at a naked Australian woman. She bore a striking resemblance to American women. She had two arms, two legs, two breasts, a furry patch between her legs, and smooth, white skin. Naked, she no longer appeared chubby, but simply full bodied.

She moved toward him then, totally naked, and unbuttoned his shirt. Together they removed his shirt, and then she helped him off with his boots and socks. After that she slid his pants down, and removed his shorts.

They stood facing each other, both naked, bodies barely touching. He put his hands on her shoulders, just to test the feel and temperature of her flesh. It was smooth and warm, and he continued to move his fingers down, over the upper portions of her bosom. Her breasts were firm and full, with heavy, rounded undersides, and he ran his fingers underneath them, deliberately skirting her nipples.

She slid her hands up over his hard, flat belly to his chest, where she made circles with her palms. She, too, was deliberately avoiding his nipples.

He closed his hands over her breasts then, hefting them from underneath, then ran his hands around to her back. With one hard, flat palm he traced the graceful curve of her spine until he encountered the slopes of her buttocks. He brought his other hand down then and closed each over a firm, rounded cheek.

She moved her hands up his chest and wound them around his neck, then pulled his head down so she could kiss him. They kissed gently at first, then their mouths opened and their tongues touched, just a gentle meeting of the nerves. He pulled her close to him and the last open space between them disappeared.

She felt his hard column of flesh between them, burning her skin.

He felt her hard nipples against his chest as she pushed her breasts against him. She began to grind herself against him, then, and the kiss continued and deepened.

Finally he broke the kiss and lifted her up into his arms.

"I'm heavy," she said, her mouth working against the side of his neck.

"You're not," he said.

He carried her to the bed, lowered her to it, and sat beside her.

"You have a beautiful body," he said. It was, too. Full and firm in breast and thigh, smooth skin, belly not flat, but not flabby, just the right amount of curve to it.

"I was about to tell you the same thing," she said stroking him up and down lightly. "This thing is like a tree," she added happily.

"Think you can chop it down?"

"I don't want to," she said, leaning over. "I want it to stay hard and get harder." Her hair, long and silky, fell across his lap, and the heat of her mouth covered the tip of his penis. He put his hand on the back of her neck as her head dipped lower and more of him slid into her mouth. She reached for his balls and cupped them gently as she started to ride his shaft up and down with her mouth, moaning. He ran his hand down the strong line of her back until he could slide his middle finger along the crack between her buttocks.

He brought his legs up onto the bed, and without releasing him from her mouth they changed positions so that his face was level with her fragrant womanhood. He slid one finger down her slit and found it very wet. He found her clit and used his finger to move it in a circular motion. Her hips twitched and she moaned again, grasping the base of his penis with one hand.

He brought his face right down to her and brushed her with his nose, then his mouth. He kissed her, getting his mouth wet, and then licked the wetness off, tasting her. It was good enough to send him back for more—in a big way.

He drove his tongue into her and she groaned, releasing him from her mouth so she could moan aloud. His penis glistened from her saliva, and grew cool as the air hit it.

"God!" she said, and licked the length of him, up and down. He continued to lick her, as well, lapping at her like a hungry cat.

"Jesus!" she whispered, moving her hips, bringing them up against his face.

When his tongue touched her clit she jumped as if struck by lightning. She took hold of his penis and once again slid a goodly portion of it into her mouth. Furiously, she began to suck him, and as he flicked her clit with his tongue he knew that she was trying to make him climax before he could make her.

He also knew she had no prayer of winning that race.

He slid one finger into her, then two, and then began to circle her clit with his tongue, faster and faster. Her hips began to twitch and he felt her belly tremble, and knew the race was over.

"Mmmmm," she moaned, but refused to let him slide free. She began to groan and moan around his penis, and the vibrations it caused seemed to be just what was needed to start him ejaculating into her mouth. She sucked and swallowed while riding out her own orgasm, and when she finally released him, she smiled and licked her lips.

"Want to rest?" she asked.

"What do you think?"

She looked at his penis, which was still hard, and licked off a drop of semen that was sitting on top like a lonely pearl.

"No, I guess not."

EIGHTEEN

"Clint?" she asked later.

"Hmm?" She was lying in the crook of his arm, and he had one hand around one of her breasts, with his eyes closed as he stroked it.

"Is it true that in your country you're a legend?"

He opened his eyes.

"Where did you hear that?"

"Jack told Enid."

"Don't listen to what Jack says," Clint said. "He likes to tell stories."

"Then you're not a legend in America."

"No," he said. "I hope you're not disappointed."

"I'm not disappointed," she said, reaching beneath the sheet to close her hand over him, "but I think you're about to become a legend in Australia."

After he finished showing Mary what a legend he was he told her he had to go out for a couple of minutes.

As he walked to the door she said, "Aren't you going to put on any clothes?"

"No," he said, "I'm just going down the hall."

He went into the hall and walked down to Jack's room. When he reached the door he heard the cries coming from inside and took a perverse pleasure in knocking rather loudly.

The cries subsided, to be replaced by a man's voice cursing as it came closer to the door.

Jack Forster appeared in the doorway, buck naked, and he had enough hair on his chest for Clint to grab it and pull him into the hall.

"What the —"

"We have to talk."

"Now?" Jack asked, annoyed.

"Shut up and listen," Clint said, showing that he was even more annoyed than Jack was. "One of the reasons I'm here in your country, Jack, is because nobody knows me."

"So?"

"I want to keep it that way."

"Why are you—"

"Don't go telling people I'm a legend, Jack," Clint said, tightly, "not even if it's a woman you want to impress. Tell as many stories about yourself as you like, but don't tell any about me. If you do, I'll be on the next boat back to America."

"J-a-a-ck-ie," Enid's voice called from inside the room.

Both Jack and Clint looked into the room and saw Enid on the bed. Her back was arched and her hand was busy between her legs.

"Oooh, Jack, come on!"

"All right," Jack said to Clint, "I'm sorry. It won't happen again."

"It better not."

Clint started down the hall to his own room when Jack called out, "Clint?"

"Yeah?" Clint said, stopping at his door.

"Don't be mad, okay?"

"Ja-a-ack!" Enid called, her tone urgent.

"You'd better get inside," Clint said, and entered his own room.

"What was that all about?" Mary asked as Clint slid back into bed.

"I just had to get something straight with my partner," he said.

"Well, now it's my turn, then."

"You're turn for what?"

She groped for him and said, "Come and get something straight for me!"

In the morning Clint woke, feeling a pleasant fatigue in his legs. He turned to look at Mary and found that she had gone. He was annoyed that she'd been able to quit the bed and leave without waking him. Even though he was in a strange country, where nobody knew who he was, that was no reason to get careless.

He was going to have to watch himself carefully. Strange country or no, men were still men, and dead was still dead.

NINETEEN

They began the four-day trip the next morning, after saying good-bye to the two girls.

Clint had to agree with Jack. He *had* gotten himself a fine-looking horse, built more for stamina than for speed. The pack horse was not quite in the same shape, but he'd make the trip, all right.

Before they left, Clint took out his gun and strapped it on. Jack preferred to carry a rifle. Jack told Clint that they could run into all kinds of dangerous creatures, including some Indians that he referred to as aborigines. It was safer for them to go armed. Clint didn't argue. He felt a hundred percent better having his gun on his hip.

As they traveled the first day, Clint saw that the terrain did resemble some areas of the United States, but then, why shouldn't it? Dirt was dirt, rocks were rocks, and trees were trees—although there were some species of trees and bushes that he had never seen before.

He also saw some creatures he'd never seen before, which Jack told him were marsupials. This meant that their young were born immature and carried around in a pouch by the mother until they were able to get around on their own.

Jack pointed out a kangeroo; a wallaby, which was like a smaller cousin of the kangeroo; and then a few koalas which looked like bears. Clint was most impressed by the kangeroo, and the speed with which the creature could jump.

When they camped that night, Clint took care of the horses while Jack made the fire and put on the coffee.

Over coffee, Jack apologized again.

"I'm sorry about yesterday. I guess I did say too much to Enid to impress her."

"Forget it," Clint said.

"I guess I didn't understand that one of the reasons you came here was to get away from your reputation."

"What do you know about my reputation?"

"I asked around about you before we left. I know they call you the Gunsmith, and that they say you're the fastest gun alive."

Clint did not respond.

"I also know that you've killed over a hundred men in gunfights."

"Jesus," Clint said, shaking his head.

"Isn't that true?"

"No," Clint said. "Very little of a man's reputation is true."

"Why do you say that?"

"Because once it *becomes* a reputation it just continues to grow and grow," Clint explained, "no matter what the man does."

"Don't most men enjoy having a reputation?"

"I can't speak for most men, Jack. I found it to be less than an advantage."

"So now you want to see what it would be like to lose it?"

"No," Clint said, thinking back. "I want to see what it would have been like never to have had it."

They drank their coffee and ate canned peaches in silence after that.

"Well," Jack finally said, breaking the silence, "I'm looking forward to finding out what it's going to be like to be rich."

"What about your wife?"

"What about her?"

"Well, excuse me if I mention it, but I've found you to be less than a faithful husband."

"Hell, I've been gone eight months," Jack said. "Do you think she's been faithful to me?"

"Are there men out where she is?"

"There are enough."

"Aren't you afraid that she might not be there when we get there?"

Jack thought it over a moment.

"No, she'll be there."

"What makes you so sure?"

"Because she's not stupid. She knows I left to get rich, and if I don't come back rich, I'll come back with an idea of how to get that way. When she hears my idea she'll decide whether she wants to stay or not. She's not going to take a chance on me getting rich and her not being there."

"That's kind of cynical."

"You don't have to be American to be cynical."

"I guess not."

TWENTY

On the second day Clint's Australian education continued.

He saw a numbat, which had 52 teeth and dined on termites; a Tasmanian devil, a small black beast which was a terror on henhouses; a nightcat and a tiger cat, neither of which was truly a cat, but relatives of the Tasmanian devil; and toward the end of the day Jack pointed out a wombat, which was a chunky, fuzzy animal that slept during the day.

That night, when they camped, Jack got curious again about Clint.

"Are you really good with that gun?" he asked, indicating the gun on Clint's hip.

"Good enough."

"What kind of answer is that?"

"It's the kind of answer that goes with the question," Clint said a bit testily. He'd been asked that question so many times during his life, and it usually preceded his having to prove the point. "What do you mean, am I really good? What does good mean?"

"I mean are you accurate as well as fast?"

"I generally hit what I'm pointing at."

"You mean what you're aiming at, don't you?"

"You aim a rifle," Clint said, "with a handgun you just point at what you want to hit."

"I never could shoot with a handgun," Jack said. "I'm pretty good with a rifle, but I never was able to master a handgun."

"Most men don't master it."

"Well, I can't hit anything with it, either," Jack said. "Would you teach me?"

Clint looked at him.

"If you're good with a rifle, why do you want to learn how to use a handgun?"

"Who knows?" Jack said, with a shrug. "I might go back to America someday. Don't you think it's good for a man to be able to use a handgun in America?"

"Tell me something," Clint said.

"What?"

"You ever kill?"

"I've shot my fair share of game," Jack said. "Even got a croc once."

"A croc?"

"A crocodile. Plenty of them in the water out here. They move pretty fast when they're on land, too."

"I meant a man," Clint said. "Have you ever killed a man with a gun?"

"No."

"Well, a rifle is what you need then," Clint said, "to kill your crocodile. A handgun is usually used to kill another man."

"If you're accurate with it," Jack said, "as accurate as you say, you could probably kill a croc with it. Have you ever seen a croc?"

"No."

"Lord, they're scary-looking things. Supposed to be descended from the dinosaurs—and that's what they look like, low-to-the-ground dinosaurs."

In spite of himself, Clint was becoming interested in seeing one of these creatures.

"How are they different from alligators?" Clint had seen a few alligators in his time.

"Scarier. A croc is brown, has a blunter snout than an alligator. Crocs are tougher-looking, uglier. I never saw them take each other on, but I'd bet on the croc."

They drank their coffee for a while and ate some fruit, and then Jack said, "I'll make you a proposition."

"What?"

"When we get to my ranch you'll teach me how to use a handgun."

"And in return?"

"I'll show you a croc," Jack said, as if he sensed Clint's interest. He leaned foward and said, "I'll get you right close up to one, close enough that you could count his teeth."

"You can do that?" Clint asked. "Get close to a creature like that?"

Jack grinned and took out his huge knife.

87

"I killed one with this once."

"Really?"

"But not before he gave me this."

Jack rolled up his right pants leg and showed Clint the scar on his calf. Clint hadn't noticed it the previous night, when they were both naked in the hall.

"Came out of the water to get me, almost took my damned leg off, but I got the bastard," Jack said with satisfaction. "I'll show you where it happened, and I'm sure his friends will be there."

Clint thought it over briefly and then said, "All right, it's a deal."

Jack laughed happily and put his knife away.

"I want something else, though."

"What?"

"One of those pig-stickers."

"One of what?"

"Maybe you'd call it a croc-sticker."

"Oh, you mean the knife? You want one of these?"

"Yes."

"All right," Jack said, "all right, then, we've got a deal."

When he thought about it, Clint figured he had to see a crocodile. Here he was in Australia, with the opportunity, and who knew if he'd ever get the same chance again.

While he was here, he wanted to try everything this strange country had to offer, so that if and when he decided to go back—and he was pretty sure he'd go back sooner or later—he would have taken all Australia had to give him.

TWENTY-ONE

On the third day Clint saw some more of Australia's inhabitants.

He saw Brumbies, wild horses that were hunted for food and sometimes captured and broken for riding; cattle and wild buffalo, which looked pretty much the same as they did in America.

Jack pointed out a dingo, a wild, yellow dog used by the aborigines for hunting.

There were flying foxes, which were not foxes but bats, and plenty of rabbits.

When they camped that night Clint found out more about Jack's ranch.

"It's small, to say the least," Jack said. "We run a few cattle, but I don't think we're ever going to get rich off of it—that is, until *we* strike it rich with gold. Then I can buy some real cattle and maybe end up with a real working ranch."

"Who's working the ranch while you're gone?"

"I had some men working for me, and they were still there when I left. I made one of them foreman, although there's not much to be foreman of—yet."

Again, Clint began to have his doubts about whether or not there'd be anyone there when they got there, or if there'd even be a ranch. If he owned a ranch he'd never stay away from it for eight months, even if he was in the *same* country.

"You leave any friends behind?" Clint asked.

"Some acquaintances and neighbors," Jack said, "but not many friends."

"Why is that?" Clint asked. "You seem to be a pretty friendly fellow."

"A by-product of being a stranger in your country," Jack said, smiling. "Being a stranger in a strange country, I learned to *be* friendly."

"Is that what you suggest I do here?"

"No need," Jack said, grinning again. "You have me."

Clint wondered just how much of an advantage that really was.

On the afternoon of the fourth day they rode into Bathurst. It wasn't much of a town. The temperature was above eighty and everything was pretty dry and dusty—including Clint and Jack.

"How far from town is your ranch?"

"Another couple of hours," Jack said, "but I'd rather stop here for a drink. What about you?"

"A beer would be fine."

That was something else Clint noticed was different about Australia—the beer—but he really hadn't been able to pinpoint the difference yet.

"I hope it's cold," he said.

"That's a vain hope," Jack said. "The best we can hope for is wet."

"I guess that'll do."

They rode to the front of a saloon and dismounted. Clint looked around, squinting his eyes against the dust that the hot wind was stirring up. There weren't many people on the streets, although he could see that the stores were all open for business, because they had their front doors wide open.

"Does it get warmer than this?"

"In the summer, but not now."

"Good," Clint said. "For some reason it feels a lot hotter than it is."

"It's dry. Let's go inside and get that drink."

Clint found that Jack was right. The beer was wet, but it was warm. Still, it cut the dust going down and that was the whole point.

The place had three or four men in it when they entered, and they got the bartender's attention immediately.

"You been away a long time, Jack," the bartender said to Jack.

"I sure have, Cyrus."

"Come back rich, like you wanted to?"

"No, but I came back knowing how to get rich."

"That's good," the man said, "not that you need it."

"Everybody needs money, Cyrus," Jack said.

"I guess so," the bartender said, and wandered down the bar to take care of another customer.

Clint wondered what the bartender meant by that, but since Jack didn't ask, he didn't, either.

A little over two hours later they pulled up within sight of a ranch with a large, sprawling house.

"Well," Clint said, "your neighbors seem to be doing well, Jack. How far are we from your house?"

When he received no answer he looked at Jack, who was staring at the house before them.

"Jack?"

"Yeah?"

"Where's your place?"

"That—" Jack said, stopping and then starting again. "That's my place."

"That's your place?" Clint asked.

Clint looked again. It was not as large as some of the large ranches he'd seen in Texas and Montana, but it certainly was not the "small" place that Jack had described to him.

"I guess I've discovered another facet of your personality, Jack."

"What's that?"

"Your flair for underestimation."

"No, Clint, you don't understand," Jack said. "This is my place, but that's not my house. I've never seen that house before in my life."

"Well, then, whose house is it?"

"I don't know."

They stared at the house in silence for a few moments and then Clint said, "Well, we're not going to find out sitting here, are we?"

He started down toward the house, and several seconds later a confused Jack Forster started after him.

TWENTY-TWO

They rode through the entrance arch and up to the house, where they dismounted in time to be met by a man who was at least as large as Jack was, maybe a touch heavier.

Before reaching the house Jack pulled alongside Clint and said, "This is my place, Clint. I recognize that clump of trees over there and that big white rock."

"Could your wife have sold the place?"

"Definitely not. It's in my name."

"Well, we'll find out what's going on soon enough."

Clint looked and saw that both the trees and the rock were distinctive enough to stand out as landmarks.

Now the big man meeting them said, "Can I help you blokes?" His tone had an edge to it, a belligerent edge that Clint knew would not stand well with the man who actually owned the place—or the land, anyway.

"Yeah, friend," Jack said, planting his feet, "you could tell me who you are."

"I think you've got this wrong, fella," the other man said. "I belong here, you don't."

"The hell I don't," Jack said. "I own the place."

A grin split the other big man's face and he said, "This place is owned by Megan Forster."

"This place is owned by *Jack* Forster," Jack said, "and that's me."

Just then the front door opened and a woman called out, "What's wrong, Pike?"

"Nothing I can't handle, love," the man called Pike replied. He looked at Jack then and said, "Jack Forster's dead, friend."

"No I ain't, friend," Jack said. "At least, not so's you'd notice."

There was a pause during which the woman came out onto the porch. Clint looked up at her and saw her looking at Jack. She was a tall, full-bodied, handsome woman of about thirty, with long chestnut hair. She was wearing a man's workshirt and jeans, and she made them look like Paris originals.

"Jack?" Clint said.

Jack and Pike had been engaging in a staring duel, and now Jack looked at Clint, then up the steps.

"Megan?" he said. "Meggie?"

The woman looked at Jack, frowned, and said, "Jack? Is that you?"

"Meggie!"

Jack ran up the steps and roughly embraced the woman,

sweeping her off her feet. Clint switched his gaze to the man called Pike, who was not looking at the tableau with any sort of enjoyment.

"Jack, put me down!" the woman yelled.

He did as she said and she straightened herself out, looking down the steps at Pike, and then at Clint.

"Meggie, tell this ocker who I am, will you?"

Megan looked down at Pike and said, "Mr. Pickett, this is my husband, Jack Forster." She looked at Jack and added, "Home after a year!" and slapped him across the face.

Jack stood stunned as the woman turned and walked back into the house, then he turned and looked down the steps at Clint.

"Welcome home, huh?" he said, and followed the woman into the house.

Clint looked at the man who had been called alternately "Pike," and "Mr. Pickett," who was still staring at the closed door of the house.

"Where can I put the horses?" he asked.

The man reluctantly pulled his eyes away from the house. "What?"

"Where can I put the horses?"

The man tossed one more glance at the house and then said, "Follow me."

He followed him to a large barn.

"You can put them inside."

"Thanks," Clint said. "My name is Adams, Clint Adams."

The man looked him up and down for a moment, eyes lingering on the gun on his hip, and then said, "Eddie Pickett. Some call me Pike."

"I'll call you Mr. Pickett," Clint said, "until you say otherwise."

"You friends with Forster?"

Clint shrugged and said, "You could say that."

"Is he planning on staying?"

"He owns the place, doesn't he?"

"He thinks he can just come waltzing back after a year?"

"He told me it was eight months."

"More like a year, but either way I don't see how he thinks—"

"I don't know what he thinks," Clint said. "I only concentrate on what I think."

"Yeah," Pickett said.

"See you later," Clint said.

"Sure."

As Pickett started walking away Clint couldn't help but ask.

"Hey?"

"Yeah?"

"What's an 'ocker'?"

"I think in your country you call them hillbillies," Pickett answered.

"How did you know where I'm from?"

Pickett grinned.

"I know an American when I hear one."

Clint let the man walk away then and took the horses in the barn.

TWENTY-THREE

When Clint entered the house he heard the raised voices of Jack and Megan Forster and followed them. After all, he and Jack were supposed to be partners.

He found them in what looked like an office, going nose to nose.

"—hell makes you think you can just come back and be welcome?" Megan was saying.

"Welcome?" Jack replied. "How can I not be welcome in my own home?"

"Your home?" she shouted. "You left me in a humpy. Does

this look like a humpy to you? I built this, not you."

"Maybe you built the house," Jack said, "but the land is mine, the cattle—"

"Cattle? You left me with twenty cows. Twenty! Now I have a thousand. They're mine!"

"We're married, Megan. What's yours is mine."

They glared at each other until they noticed Clint watching.

"Clint, come on in," Jack said. "I want you to meet my wife."

Clint entered the room.

"Megan, this is my friend, Clint Adams," Jack said. "He's my friend and my partner."

"Partner?"

"Yes."

She looked at Clint and said, "Hello. I—I apologize for my behavior. You're a guest in my house."

"Our house," Jack said.

"Uh, you two have a lot to talk about," Clint said, starting to back out.

"Wait," Megan said, moving away from Jack. "I'll show you to your room. I'm sure you want to get cleaned up after your long journey."

"Uh, yes, a bath would be nice."

She turned to Jack and said, "We can talk later, Jack."

"Sure," Jack said. "After you show Clint to his room, you can show me where ours is."

"Ours—" she said, but cut herself short. "We'll talk later." To Clint she said, "Come this way."

She walked past him into the hall. He threw a glance at Jack and then followed her.

She led him down the hall into the entry foyer and then up

a flight of stairs. In the upstairs hall she led him to a door and then turned to face him.

"Here's your room. Downstairs behind the steps is a room with a bath. I will have a bath drawn for you by one of the servants."

"You're very kind."

"I'm not usually such a shrew," she said, patting her hair, which looked fine to him. "I—Jack's coming back has thrown me off balance. You understand."

"I understand."

She was not at all what he had expected. He'd expected someone much younger, not as self-possessed or obviously intelligent. Up close he saw that she had wonderfully large brown eyes and full lips.

"Are you and Jack friends?" she asked.

"That's the second time I've been asked that question."

"Pike?"

He nodded.

"What did you tell him?"

"I said you could say that."

"But you're partners?"

Clint grinned.

"Don't worry, Mrs. Forster," he said. "I'm not going to be looking for a piece of all this."

"I'm sorry. I didn't mean—"

"Don't apologize," he said. "It's not necessary."

She smiled at him—the first time he'd seen her smile—and said, "Thank you. I'll see to that bath."

"Thanks."

She started back down the hall and he called out, "Mrs. Forster?"

She turned and said, "Call me Megan."

"All right . . . Megan."

"What did you want to ask me?"

"What's a humpy?"

She grinned again and said, "A humpy is a shack."

He looked at the ceiling and said, "This sure as hell is no humpy."

"I know," she said. "That's my whole point."

TWENTY-FOUR

Clint enjoyed a long, leisurely, hot bath, attended by a girl servant named Jean. She was barely eighteen, apparently shy, as she averted her eyes whenever she added a bucket of water to the bath. She had very dark skin and black hair and was very lovely.

Clint wondered what the outcome of Jack and Megan Forster's dilemma would be. Apparently in Jack's absence Megan had been able to build the ranch up to this level. Clint was looking forward to learning just how she accomplished it.

But that left a great problem for them to resolve. Jack owned the land, but did he still own the ranch?

And what was Pickett's place in all this? From Clint's observations, he knew that Pickett did not like the idea that Jack—Megan's husband—had returned. He obviously had very strong feelings for her, but were those feelings returned? And if they were, could she be blamed? After all, her husband had been away a year. What woman could wait that long without transferring her needs to another?

And what of that? Had Jack lied when he had made it eight months, or had he simply lost count of how long he'd been gone?

"A towel," Clint said to the girl.

"Yes."

She brought him a towel and as he stood up to dry himself, instead of looking away, she stared at him.

"Haven't you ever seen a naked man before?" he asked, amused.

"Yes," she said, "but not a white man."

Just then there was a knock on the door, and she averted her eyes hastily.

"Come in," Clint said, putting the towel around his waist.

The door opened and Megan Forster walked in. If she expected Clint to be dressed she showed no surprise that he wasn't.

"If you're finished with your bath, dinner will be served in half an hour."

"I'll be ready."

"I will send Jean to your room to show you the way."

"That's fine."

Megan nodded, and left the room.

Clint dressed while Jean busied herself emptying the tub

and tending to the wet towels.

"Well, Jean, I'll see you in a little while," he said, preparing to leave the room.

"Yes, sir," she said. "I will come for you when dinner is ready."

"Thanks for your help."

She nodded, and continued with her duties.

Clint left the room and ran into Jack upstairs.

"Had your bath?" Jack asked.

"Yes. I feel a lot better."

Jack looked as if he had bathed, as well.

As if reading Clint's mind he said, "I took a bath in my room."

"Your room?" Clint asked.

"Sure, the master bedroom," Jack said. "It's just down at the end of the hall."

"Have you and . . . your wife resolved anything?"

"We've resolved that I'm back," Jack said.

"Is she going to accept that?"

"Why wouldn't she?"

"Well . . . you have to admit she hasn't exactly welcomed you back with open arms."

"Ah," Jack said, waving that away with his hand, "that's just her way. Believe me, she's glad I'm back . . . and even if she's not," he added, giving Clint a conspiratorial elbow, "she will be after tonight, eh?"

"If you say so."

"Come on, get dressed for dinner. Megan tells me she—we—have a wonderful cook."

Clint watched him hightail it down the hall and thought how out of place Jack looked in a house this size.

Jack Forster was more suited to a humpy.

Clint was the last one down to dinner, and as he entered the dining room—following the lovely young Jean—Megan told the cook she could serve dinner.

At the table was Megan, Jack, Clint, and Pickett.

"Why is he here?" Jack asked.

"I thought you two should meet," she said. "After all, he's foreman."

"What happened to Willis?"

Megan made a face.

"Willis left a month after you did, Jack, after I refused to let him in my bed."

Dinner was all kinds of vegetables with dark, tender, juicy meat which Clint was afraid to ask the name of. He didn't want to find out that he was eating a horse—even though that's what he thought.

After dinner the cook brought out a large pot of coffee and poured for everyone.

"All right, Gladys," Megan said. "I think we can do without you now."

"Yes, ma'am."

After she left, Megan said, "We have to work this out, Jack."

"I don't think he should be here," Jack said, pointing at Pickett.

"Well, I don't think he should be here," Pickett said, indicating Clint.

"He's my guest," Jack said.

"I'm the foreman."

"You may not be anymore."

"Why you—" Pickett said, throwing down his napkin and getting to his feet.

"That's enough!" Megan shouted before Jack could get up as well. "Sit down, Pike," she said. When he didn't do it right away she said, "Damn it, sit!" and he sat.

"Jack," she said, "you own part of this land."

"Part. What do you mean—"

"Just listen," she said. "When you left you left me with a humpy and ten acres. Now there's this house, and over two hundred acres."

"Two hundred?" Jack said.

"That's right, and maybe more to come."

"Well, honey, where did all the money come from for this?"

"Well, now, that's something that we have to talk about in private."

"Well, let's go, then—"

"Tomorrow, Jack, tomorrow. I have to get used to having you here, first."

"Well, I'm all for that," Jack said, starting to rise. "Let's get to it."

Clint noticed that the remark didn't sit too well with Pickett, who started to push his chair back.

"Hey, Pickett," Clint said, "why don't you show me around while we've still got some daylight."

"What?" Pickett asked, distracted.

"Show me around."

"Yes, that's a very good idea, Pike," Megan said. "Why don't you show Clint around."

"Megan—"

"Jack and I have to talk," she said, and she was staring at him hard.

Clearly unhappy, Pickett stood up and said, "All right, Adams, let's go."

Clint looked at Jack and Megan and said, "If you'll excuse me . . . " and followed Pickett.

TWENTY-FIVE

Outside Clint said, "All right, Pickett. We can stop the tour right here."

"What?"

"I just wanted to make sure you and Jack didn't break the furniture."

Pickett sort of hesitated in his tracks, then relaxed and leaned against the side of the house.

"That lady in there seems very much in control."

"She is."

"How do you feel about that?"

"This is her place. She's the boss."

Clint decided not to come right out and ask Pickett about him and Megan Forster.

"How long have you worked here?"

"Six months."

"Before or after she hit it rich?"

"Just after," he said, "when she decided that she really did need a foreman."

"How did she hit it rich, Pickett?"

Pickett looked at Clint and took a moment to light a cigar.

"I don't really know," he said. "I know she struggled for some time after her husband . . . left . . . and then suddenly she started acquiring land and stock and she needed somebody to manage it."

"Who manages her money?"

"She does."

Clint shook his head.

"I tell you, she sure isn't what I expected after talking to Jack."

"She's never what anyone expects. She's one tough lady, and fair."

"And beautiful."

Pickett gave him a quick look, then said, "Yeah, and that, too."

"I'm not going to tell you that now, Jack," Megan said again. "I want to resolve the rest of this first."

"The rest of what?" Jack demanded. "I want to know where all the money came from."

"Where it came from doesn't matter," she said. "It's mine."

"And this place is mine."

"No, it's not," she said.

"What do you mean?"

"You may not realize this, Jack, but this house doesn't stand where your humpy did."

"What?"

"You built your shack on the edge of your ten acres. Well, when I tore it down and built this house, I moved it off your original ten acres. The land that this house is standing on is in my name, not yours."

"Wait a minute," he said. "We're married."

"That's what we have to talk about."

"What about it?"

"I don't want to be married to you anymore."

"What do you mean, not be married to me anymore? What are you talking about. We *are* married."

"You call what we are married?" she asked. "Two months after our wedding day you disappear and show up again after a year?"

"I went off to get rich."

"You didn't have to leave the country to do that."

"Obviously," he said. "You did it without leaving."

"I'm not rich."

"Well, if you aren't, you're putting on a pretty good act."

"I'm doing well, very well, and I don't think I should have to share it with you just because we recited some vows fourteen months ago."

"So that's it. You don't want to share."

"Obviously those vows meant very little to you."

"What are you—"

"Jack, I caught you with that little tramp—"

"I explained that—"

111

"To *your* satisfaction," she said. "Don't tell me that the whole year you've been gone you've been faithful."

"Megan—"

"Look, I'll make a deal with you," she said.

"What?"

"You have your ten acres," she said. "I'll give you forty more, and some of the cattle—"

"I don't want charity, Megan," he said. "I want what's mine"

"That's ten acres and twenty cows, Jack."

"No," he said, "we're married, and what's yours is mine."

"It's not going to be like that, Jack," she said. "I've worked too hard for all of this to just give away half of it."

"You won't have to give it away," he said. "In fact, I'll be able to buy it from you with no problem, not that I should have to buy what's mine."

"What do you mean?"

"I mean that pretty soon I *will* be rich, and not just well-off, like you."

"Well, I hope so."

He stood up from the table and said, "Just wait and see."

"And what does Clint have to do with all this?"

"Clint?" he said. "You have no idea who he is, do you?"

"Only from what you've said, and what he's said . . . " she said, puzzled. "Why, who is he?"

"Well, he certainly wouldn't tell you this himself, but I'll tell you, because I want you to see what kind of a friend and partner I've got. . . . "

TWENTY-SIX

Outside, Clint ended up getting a somewhat informal look at the grounds as he and Pickett walked around.

"When do you think we should go back in?" Clint asked idly.

"I'm not going back in," Pickett said. "I'll talk to Megan tomorrow."

"You call your boss by her first name, huh?"

"Sure," he said, "and she calls me Pike."

"Where'd that come from?"

He shrugged.

"Short for Pickett, I guess. They used to call me that when I was a kid."

"Who calls you that now?"

"Just Megan."

Clint nodded. How would she know his childhood nickname if they weren't involved?

"Goodnight, Adams," Pickett said, and headed for the bunkhouse.

Clint wondered if he usually slept in the bunkhouse, or with the boss?

He decided he'd keep a sharp eye on Eddie Pickett. The man looked as though he could be dangerous.

Clint went inside and met Megan walking through the entry hall.

"Oh," she said, stopping short as he entered. "I was just going to the office to do some work."

"You usually work in the evening?"

"It's quiet," she said. "That's what I need to do paperwork."

Clint nodded, and they stood there awkwardly, wondering whether to say something or simply go their separate ways.

"Did Pike show you around?"

"I was very impressed by what I saw."

"I'm glad. I've worked very hard for this."

"I'm sure you have. You have every reason to be proud, and protective of what you own."

"I only wish that . . . certain others felt the same way."

"Speaking of Jack, where is he?"

"Uh, Jack went upstairs, I think," she said.

Clint nodded.

"His room is right next to yours."

And not at the end of the hall. He was not sharing the master bedroom with her, as he led Clint to believe.

"I see."

"Well, I'll see you in the morning, then. If you need anything, you can ask Jean. She has been instructed to look after your needs."

"Jean," he said. "She's very interesting."

"Yes. That's not her real name, of course, but it's what we call her."

"What is her real name?"

Megan laughed.

"You wouldn't be able to pronounce it."

"She's kind of quiet, isn't she?"

"Yes."

"Where is she from?"

"The outback. She's an aborigine."

"An Indian?"

"You could call her that, yes."

"And the outback? What is that?"

"It's a dry, desert area. It actually covers over forty percent of Australia. It's very difficult to live in, and only the aborigines would survive."

"I see. Well, thanks for everything, Mrs. Forster."

"Megan."

"Yes, Megan. I know this must be trying for you—"

"Having you here is not trying at all, Clint," she said. "Goodnight."

She went down the hall to her office and he went upstairs.

In her office, Megan Forster sat behind her desk and closed her eyes. She remembered a time when she would go to sleep at night hoping that when she woke up, her husband would be home.

She remembered a time when she wished that she would receive word that he was dead.

She remembered loving him.

She remembered hating him.

Now, she felt nothing for him.

Before she could think about that, though, she had to resolve the problem of Jack. . . .

And then there was her other problem, the one which still had to take precedence over everything else.

Someone was killing her stock, tearing down her fences, just generally making a nuisance of themselves, preventing any of her workdays from going smoothly.

Someone . . . and she thought she knew who that someone was.

She also thought she knew who could help her.

She admitted to herself that she had already found Jack's friend Clint interesting, but now, after what Jack had told her about this famed American gunman, he was even more interesting.

Maybe this "Gunsmith" was just the man she needed to help solve her major problem, if he would agree.

Maybe . . . if she asked him real nice, he would.

As he approached his room, the door next to his opened and Jack stepped out. When he saw Clint he pulled the door shut behind him.

"Just checking out some of the other rooms."

"Uh-huh."

"I'll want to be off early in the morning, Clint," Jack said.

"Off?"

"Yeah. I don't think we should waste any time not looking for gold, do you?"

"Uh, no, I guess not."

"I know just the areas to look in, too, so be ready."

"I'll be ready."

"All right. See you later."

"If I don't, then I'll bid you goodnight now," Clint said.

"Goodnight?" Jack said. "It's too early to turn in. I'm going to Bathurst. You want to come along?"

"No, I think I'll stay here. I'm not as young as I used to be."

"Ahh," Jack said, "go on. I'll see you early in the morning."

Clint opened his door, stepped in, and stopped short when he saw Jean on his bed.

"Mrs. Forster said I was to see to your needs," she said, and she seemed prepared to do so to the utmost.

She was naked.

TWENTY-SEVEN

He closed the door behind him and walked to the foot of the bed.

"Jean, I'm very flattered, but—"

"You do not want me?" she asked, pulling the sheet up to her neck.

"It's not that," he said. "You're lovely, but you don't have to—"

"If you send me away I will be disgraced," she said.

"Jean, please don't get the wrong idea. You're a lovely girl, and any man would want you—"

"But you do not?"

He tried to think of a way to put it that wouldn't insult her.

"I'd be glad to share my bed with you," he said, finally, "as long as I knew it was something you wanted as much as I did."

"I am here," she said. "Is that not enough?"

To illustrate her point she unwrapped her blanket and let it drop to the ground around her. Her breasts made him catch his breath. They weren't large, but they were firm, well-rounded, topped with nipples like chocolate.

"Would you like me to go?" she said. She shifted to her knees, putting herself on display. The rest of her body was as breathtaking as her breasts. Sleek and solid, she knelt there for his examination, and he had to admit that his answer to that question was an emphatic No, he certainly did not want her to leave.

He moved toward her, palming her breasts, thumbing her nipples.

"Can you answer a question for me?" he asked.

"What?"

"Do Indians kiss?"

She smiled, obviously not minding that he had called her an Indian. "This one does."

He leaned over and kissed her. Her lips were warm and pliant, and she closed her eyes. She had clearly done that before.

He kissed her neck, then her breasts, running his hands over her. He pushed her back onto the bed, undressed, and joined her. He kissed her inverted navel, and worked his way even further down. She wrapped her hands in his hair as he ran his mouth over her flat belly, then ran his tongue into the tangled black forest of her pubic hair, cupping her buttocks, and pulling her to him.

He could smell her readiness then and could wait no longer.

When he tasted her she jumped at the touch of his tongue, then sighed and reached for him, holding his head as he ran his tongue over her and inside her. Clearly she had never had this done to her before, and a small orgasm caused her to shudder.

She was wet and ready and he slid himself into her slowly, until he was in to the hilt. She wrapped her arms around him as he started to ride her, and he buried his face in her neck and hair, inhaling her fragrance. She lifted her knees and spread them, and ran her nails lightly over his back. She picked up his rhythm quickly, matched it, and then drove toward her climax with him. When it came her nails dug into his back and her breath caught in her throat. When he began to fill her with his seed she moaned and clutched at him, but surprisingly did not cry out. . . .

Later they made love again, with her on top. He played with her breasts while she rode him in obvious enjoyment, biting her lip and humming to herself, and this time they climaxed together instead of seconds apart. . . .

Clint stood at the window overlooking the front of the house while Jean slept on the bed behind him. It was only about ten o'clock, and Jack had not yet returned from Bathurst. The weight of the four-day trip was weighing heavily on Clint, and he wondered how Jack could even think about riding to Bathurst and back so soon after it.

Ah, to be young. . . .

He turned and went to the bed, slid underneath the sheet with Jean, whose body was incredibly warm. In moments, he was asleep and barely felt it when she turned in to him and pressed herself to him. From that point on they both slept peacefully.

TWENTY-EIGHT

Megan Forster woke that morning with her emotions in a jumble. Alone in bed she remembered the only good thing she and Jack had ever had, and that was sex. Last night, however, it had not been Jack she was thinking about . . . or even Pike, who had been the one she turned to recently for sex when she needed it. No, the man she'd been thinking about was Clint Adams, whose room was just down the hall.

Unfortunately, Jack's room was down the hall, too, so she had gone to sleep with her knees pressed tightly together.

Now she rose, wondering how she could get Clint alone so

that he'd listen to what she had to ask him . . . and maybe they could *really* find some time to be alone. . . .

She decided to take a cold bath before going downstairs. She went looking for Jean. . . .

Clint woke in the morning with Jean pressed warmly and tightly against his back, spoon fashion. He tried to get off the bed without waking her, but she was almost instantly awake the moment he moved.

"Good morning," he said.

She smiled, and then the smile faded.

"What time is it?"

"It's early," he said, walking to the bed. "Go back to sleep."

"I do not want to go back to sleep," she said. She reached out and stroked his penis with her fingertips, and he couldn't help but react. As it swelled she closed her small hand around it.

She slid off the bed and knelt down in front of him to kiss the head of his now erect penis. Cupping his balls gently she opened her mouth and took just the head in, sucking it, wetting it. Little by little, then, she took more and more of him inside until, cupping his buttocks now, she began to suck.

She seemed utterly fascinated with his body, a fascination he did not mind letting her explore.

She reversed her position and sat between his legs so she could lick his balls. While doing so she took hold of his penis again and found it hard and ready. She got on her knees behind him, pressing her breasts against his ass, and began to pull on his long penis with her right hand. With her left she continued to fondle his balls. She rubbed her nipples over the smooth surface of his buttocks, and her hand continued to pump him furiously. When he thought he was going to come, she released him and moved around in front of him again.

She took hold of his penis and pulled him so that he had to move onto the bed. She pushed him down onto his back and mounted him, taking him inside in one quick thrust that took away her breath—and his.

She rode him for a long time, biting her lip, her head thrown back, but still not making a sound. For some reason, Clint wanted to see if he could make her cry out. When he could feel her orgasm approaching, Clint decided to turn the tables on her, a bit. Abruptly he took her by the waist and lifted her off him. His cock, glistening with her juices, became suddenly cold. He reversed their position so that she was on her back, and then he went to work on her.

He started with her breasts, licking them gently, kissing them, sucking on the nipples, then began to kiss her neck, the hollow of her throat, behind her ears. . . .

All the while he kept his hands busy, rubbing her belly, stroking her inner thighs, rubbing his hard penis against her outer thigh. . . .

He kissed her mouth, sucked on her tongue, bit her bottom lip, kissed her chin, her neck again, her breasts, between her breasts, her belly, working all the way down until he was kissing the soft flesh of her inner thighs. He ran his tongue over her vagina, gently, teasingly, and he could feel her legs stiffen. He reached up so that he could squeeze her nipples while he licked her, and he felt a small orgasm ripple through her body, causing her to sigh, and then to moan. . . .

He allowed his tongue to enter her vagina, pushing past the glistening lips. He licked her, sucked at her noisily, worked his tongue up to her rigid clit. He closed his mouth over it, sucking it, and flicking it with his tongue, all the while continuing to manipulate her nipples. When he felt her belly starting to tremble he backed off, kissing her thighs, squeezing her nipples, but leaving her clit straining and rigid. She lifted her hips in an effort to get his mouth back, but he continued to kiss and lick her thighs, biting her at one point gently, sucking at one point to leave a small love bruise, and then he moved back to her vagina, to her clit. . . .

. . . Finally he let her come, a shattering climax that lifted her hips off the bed. She put her hand in her mouth to keep herself from crying out, and Clint accepted that as his small victory over her.

Before the last vestiges of that orgasm could fade, he climbed atop her and entered her, violently so that she had to gasp and hold it. He began to take her in long, hard strokes, and she grabbed for him, clutching his buttocks, scraping them with her nails, until finally she came again, biting his shoulder this time to force herself to keep silent. . . .

A few minutes later he told her, "*Now* you can go back to sleep."

She shook her head and hurriedly slipped from the bed.

"I have to get to work," she said, grabbing her simple dress and putting it on. "Mrs. Forster will be looking for me." She hurried to the door, then stopped, and turned to look back at him.

"Would you like a bath this morning?" she asked.

"Is there water in that pitcher?" he asked, indicating the pitcher on the dresser by the window.

"Yes."

"Then I'll simply use that."

She neither answered, nor did she leave. He thought that she must be waiting for some sort of good-bye.

"I'll see you later, Jean."

She smiled and hurried out.

Clint went to the pitcher, poured some water into the basin and began to wash. He hoped Megan wouldn't catch Jean coming out of his room. He'd hate for the girl to lose her job simply because they'd had one hell of a memorable night— and morning—together.

TWENTY-NINE

"Good morning," Megan called out as he came down the steps.

Once again they had met in the entry way, as if some force kept their paths crossing. She looked as if she were fresh from a bath. Her skin had a well-scrubbed glow to it, and the ends of her hair were damp.

"How did you sleep?" she asked.

"Fine."

"Did Jean see to your needs?"

Clint tried to read something into the remark, but couldn't.

"Yes, she looked after me very well."

"Good. Come along, breakfast should be ready."

"Has Jack been down?"

"I don't know," she said, and her tone clearly stated that she didn't care much, either.

She went into the dining room, and he followed.

Breakfast was much like the breakfasts Clint had enjoyed in his own country. Eggs, bacon, potatoes, biscuits—all prepared to perfection.

"You have a fine cook," Clint said.

"Thank you. I—" She stopped short when Jack came out of the kitchen. "What were you doing in there?"

"Just making arrangements," he said, seating himself.

"For what?"

"A little expedition Clint and I will be going on shortly. I needed some supplies, and the cook was nice enough to cooperate."

"You probably bullied her into it."

"Maybe she just recognizes her master when she sees him," he suggested.

"Gladys works for me, not for you, Jack."

"We'll see," Jack said, and applied himself to his breakfast with vigor.

Megan looked at Clint, who held her eyes.

"Tell me about yourself, Clint."

"What do you want to know?"

"Are you married?"

"No."

"Ever been?"

"No."

"Ever been close?"

"I've been close, but . . . never took the final step."

"I see. What is it you do for a living in your country?"

"I was a lawman for a while, now I fix guns."

"Oh, a gunsmith?"

"Yes," he said. It had been a long time since anyone had said that name to him and meant nothing more by it than what it implied.

"Perhaps we might have some weapons for you to look at while you're here. Out here it's a little difficult to get them fixed once they break."

"I'd be happy to."

"We'll be busy!" Jack snapped.

Megan threw Jack a hard look, but Clint said, "I'm sure I can make time, Megan."

"Thank you."

The rest of the meal went on with only small talk exchanged between Megan and Clint. For that reason, Jack finished his breakfast first.

"I have to go upstairs for some gear, Clint," he said. "When I come back down, we can get going."

"Sure."

After Jack left Megan said, "Why did you hook up with him, Clint?"

Clint shrugged.

"We hit it off. He invited me to come home with him."

"But home was thousands of miles away. Didn't that matter to you?"

"No," Clint said, "it didn't."

"How long are you planning on staying?"

"I haven't really thought about it. I guess a lot of that will be up to you."

131

"As far as I'm concerned, you can stay here as long as you like. In fact, I'd like us to be able to spend some time together. I'd like to get to know you better."

He looked at her then and saw that she was looking at him with genuine interest.

"I'd like that, Megan," he said. "I think I'd like that quite a lot."

THIRTY

Clint went outside and saddled Duke and another horse for Jack. He didn't know how long Jack intended to stay out, but the big man had obviously made arrangements for them to have supplies along.

When Jack finally appeared, Clint was surprised at the guilt he felt over the last exchange with Megan Forster. If Jack Forster wasn't his friend, he was at least his partner, and Megan was Jack's wife. If Clint was reading Megan's words correctly, she had her eye on him rather than on her returning husband. Clint usually tried to stay away from married women—though he *had* slept with his share of them—and he especially avoided any kind of entanglements with women married to men he knew.

"All right," Jack said, reaching him, "let's get going."

"Do we need a pack animal?"

"No," Jack said, holding up a canvas sack. "This'll do it. All I want to do is go out and look around. Once I find our spot, then we can stock up on supplies to stay out a week or more. I don't want to come back until I'm rich."

Clint shrugged and mounted Duke. In front of the house he saw Pickett watching them, and then he noticed Megan watching from a front window.

Jack mounted up and tied his sack to his saddle.

"Jack, have you really resolved anything with Megan yet?"

"Yeah," Jack said, "I've resolved that she's an ungrateful bitch. I don't know how she managed to build this ranch up, but I do know that she doesn't want to share it with her loving husband."

Clint couldn't seem to find it in him to fault Megan for that, especially since he'd seen firsthand what a loving husband Jack Forster really was.

"Let's get moving," Jack said. "I can smell gold in the air."

Clint sniffed the air and smelled nothing.

He hoped he was the one who was wrong.

They had ridden for half an hour when Clint noticed the herd.

"That must be Megan's," Clint said.

Jack looked at the herd and said, "Half mine"

Clint didn't comment. There looked to be about a hundred head there, but he had no way of knowing if that was the entire herd.

"Come on," Jack said, but as he started away, Clint didn't follow. He'd spotted two men on a rise on the other side of the herd, and they were riding toward the cows.

"Hold up, Jack."

Jack reined in and turned his head to look over his shoulder. "What is it?"

"I don't know," Clint said.

Clint watched the two men carefully. Of course, he couldn't know that they weren't Megan's men, but he had a bad feeling that was verified when both men took out their rifles.

"Looks like trouble," Clint said.

"Oh, yeah?"

Suddenly, the two men raised their rifles and began to fire into the herd.

"They're killing the cows!" Clint shouted.

"Well, let them," Jack said. "We've got more important things to do."

"Jack, they're shooting Megan's herd—your herd."

"Yeah, well, maybe they'll just shoot her half."

"You can't just ride away and ignore it."

"I can't?" Jack said. "Watch me. You can stay and watch if you want, but I'm going after my gold."

Clint had no intentions of just standing and watching. As Jack rode away he wheeled Duke around and began to ride around the herd. He hoped he could reach them before they killed too many cows.

"You know I love you, Megan," Pickett said.

"Not now, Pike" Megan replied.

They were in her office and Pickett had worked up his courage to come and talk to her about Jack . . . and Clint.

"You're not going to let him stay, are you?"

"Not if I can help it," Megan said.

"Did he sleep with you last night?"

She looked at him, eyes flashing.

"That's none of your business."

"The hell it isn't," he said. "Or maybe it's not your husband you're interested in."

"What does that mean?"

"It means I saw the way you were looking at the other one—Adams."

"Even if I was looking at Clint Adams, that's none of your business, either."

"Megan—"

"You work for me, Pike!" she said, sharply. "Sometimes I let you in my bed, but that doesn't change the fact that you work for me. If you want to go on working for me you'll go out and do your job. I want some men on the herd for security."

"You think something's going to happen?"

"Something's been happening ever since I turned down Collier's offer to buy the place. So far they've been accident's, but I don't want any more accident's happening. Get the men out there to keep a watch on the cows."

"All right," he said. He turned to go to the door, then turned back. "Megan . . . I'm sorry . . . it's just that I feel. . . ."

"Pike," she said, closing her eyes, "I really can't listen to what you feel at the moment, maybe later, okay?"

"Sure," he said, "sure, maybe later."

After Pike left, Megan turned and looked out the window. From their conversation that morning she was pretty sure now that Clint was as interested in her as she was in him. When he got back, maybe she'd get to talk with him. Maybe she'd be able to get him to help.

All she had to do was to get him away from Jack. Clint might have thought that Jack was his friend, but he didn't know Jack the way she did. Jack didn't care for anyone but Jack.

She found herself worrying that Clint might get hurt by Jack, much like the way she had—though on a much smaller scale, of course.

She didn't want to see that, and would do what she could to stop it.

When the two men spotted Clint riding toward them they exchanged glances, obviously wondering who he was, or what to do. They didn't turn tail and run, because after all, he was only one man.

"Who do you think this is?" the first man asked the second.

"I don't know," the second man said, "but whoever he is, he's crazy. Look at the way he's riding at us, like there was two of him and one of us."

"Well, let's show him how wrong he is."

Both men raised their rifles, but before they could fire Clint drew and fired. The bullet hit the first man in the shoulder and knocked him off his horse.

"Jesus," the second man said, and this time he did turn tail and run, while his partner's horse took off in another direction.

"Damn you—" the man on the ground shouted, clutching his shoulder.

When Clint rode up to him, the man glared up at him with hatred.

"Lucky shot," he said to Clint.

"Lucky for you," Clint said, holstering his gun and dismounting.

"What do you mean?"

"I was aiming for your head."

Clint was walking the man back to the ranch at the end of a rope, pulling him along behind Duke when he came across three men coming from the direction of the house.

"You're the bloke what came back with Jack Forster, aren't you?" one of them asked.

"That's right."

"Who you got there?"

"That's what I'd like to find out," Clint said. "I caught him and a friend of his shooting cattle."

"Blimey," the man said. "We're on our way out there to stand guard over them."

"Well, you'll find about a half dozen dead, maybe as many as eight. Is that the entire herd?"

"Not hardly," the man said. "We'll be rounding them up in a week or so, but right now they're spread all around."

"Is someone looking after the others?"

"They're split in three more groups, and Pickett is sending men out to each," the man said. "This is the smallest section."

"Any of you know this fella?" Clint asked.

They all looked at the man who was standing behind Duke, both wrists tied. He was bleeding from the shoulder, although there had been some attempt to stem the flow with pieces torn from the man's own shirt.

"Where are you taking him?"

"Back to the ranch. I want to try and find out who he is and who he works for."

"You need one of us to ride back with you?" the spokesman asked.

"No, I think you fellas better get to that herd and protect it."

"All right then, fellas," the man said, "you heard what the man said."

The three men continued on their way, and Clint turned to look at his captive.

"Hey, you've got to let me rest."

"Are you ready to tell me who you work for?"

The man didn't answer.

"Then you better start walking," Clint said, and jerked on the man's rope.

THIRTY-ONE

Pickett was the first one to spot Clint coming back with the man dragging behind him. By the time Clint reached the house, there was a small crowd gathered, and Megan was standing on the porch.

"What have you got there?" Megan asked.

"This fella and a friend of his were killing your cattle," Clint said.

"And you stopped him?"

"Yes."

"I'll take him," Pickett said, stepping foward and reaching for the rope.

Clint did not give the man up right away.

"He refuses to tell me who he works for," he said to Megan.

"That's all right," Megan said. "I know who he works for."

"Is that so?"

She nodded.

"Give him over to Pike, Clint, and come inside. We have to talk."

Pickett still had his hand out, so Clint handed him the rope and dismounted.

A man stepped forward and said, "I'll take care of your horse for you, Mister."

"Thanks," Clint said, and handed over Duke's reins.

He went up the stairs and followed Megan into the house and down the hall to her office.

"You look like you need a drink," she said.

"I could use one."

She went to a sideboard where she had some decanters and said, "Whiskey or brandy?"

"Whiskey."

She poured him one and handed it to him.

"Now suppose you tell me what we have to talk about?" he asked.

"Sit down," she said, then added, "please."

He sat.

"Where's Jack?"

"Out looking for gold."

"Gold?"

"He thinks he can find some around here."

"I wish him luck," he said. "If he strikes it rich it will get him off my back. He didn't see what was going on with the cattle?"

"He saw."

"Did he help you?"

"No."

She frowned.

"How many men did you say there were?"

"Two."

"What happened to the other one?"

"He ran when I shot this one."

She sat back in her chair and sipped her own drink. Clint saw that she had taken the brandy.

"Clint, I know who you are."

"You do?" he asked. "Who am I?"

She told him everything that Jack had told her and saw that it made him unhappy.

"What's wrong?"

"I told Jack what would happen if he started telling people about me."

"Well, he only told me, and I haven't told anyone else."

"I'll have to leave, Megan," Clint said.

"Why"

"This isn't turning out the way I thought."

"That's my fault, I guess."

"No, it's Jack's," Clint said. "I'm usually a good judge of people, but I guess I was way off with him. Why'd you marry him, anyway?"

"I thought I loved him," she said. "No, I guess I did love him, but I didn't really get to know him until after we were married—and then he left. I hated him for leaving, but now I realize that it was the best thing that ever happened to me. I learned to fend for myself."

"And you built all of this?"

"Yes."

"You're a very impressive woman."

"Thank you, but I need your help right now."

"What kind of help?"

"The same kind of thing you did today."

"You said you knew who he worked for."

"Yes, he works for a man named John Collier."

"Who is this Collier?"

"He's a man who offered to buy my ranch from me."

"And you refused."

"As I said, I worked very hard for this."

"So he's trying to force you to sell?"

"Yes. Accidents have been happening over the past month or so. Cattle dying, apparently poisoned; fences falling down, or being pulled down."

"What happened today was a little obvious, though."

"I guess he's decided to upgrade his 'accidents'."

"What can I do?"

She leaned foward.

"I'm sorry if you're unhappy that I know who you are, but you must see that you can help me. We have no one here who is as proficient with a gun as you are, and I'm sure that Collier doesn't either. He's got a bunch of ockers working for him—bullies. They've picked fights with my men when I send them to town. They've beaten up three of my people so badly they can't work."

Clint frowned. This all sounded so familiar to him. He'd run into the same sort of thing so many times in his own country, a powerful rancher trying to spread his power, widen his holdings, and using violence to do it.

"What do you want me to do?"

"I want you to go into town with some of my men. They have to pick up some supplies. I know that some of Collier's

144

men will be waiting for them. You can show them that we won't stand for being bullied."

Clint sipped his drink and thought it over.

"I'll pay you—"

"Don't try to hire my gun, Megan," he said quickly. "If you do that I will have to leave."

"I'm sorry. I meant no offense."

"No, I know you didn't," he said, putting his glass down and standing up. "I'll help you for nothing."

"Why?"

"Because I've seen men like Collier before and I don't like them, whether they're in America or here."

"Is that the only reason?"

He walked around the desk, took hold of her upper arms, and pulled her to her feet.

"You know it isn't," he said, staring into her eyes.

Her breathing quickened and she looked very beautiful in that moment, more so than he'd seen her before.

He released her and stepped back.

"When are your men leaving?"

"In about half an hour," she said. "Tell Pike to introduce you to them. Tell him that you'll be in charge in town."

"Is he going?"

"No."

"He won't like this. He'll see me as a threat to him."

"I'll take care of Pike," she said. "You take care of Collier's men."

"I won't kill them," he said. "Not if I don't have to. I'll just discourage them a little."

"That's all I ask."

He nodded and started for the door. When he stopped and

looked back at her she was holding her upper arms where he had held her. He knew he hadn't held her tight enough to hurt her.

"I'll see you later."

She licked her lips and said, "Yes."

THIRTY-TWO

As Clint expected, Pickett wasn't happy with the turn events had taken, and he stormed over to the house to complain about it.

That left two men sitting in a buckboard looking at Clint, who was astride Duke.

"You men have a problem with this?" he asked.

"Not if Mrs. Forster doesn't," one of them said.

"We work for her," the other said.

"What are your names?"

"Jake," the first one said.

"I'm Harry."

"All right Jake and Harry, we'll go into town and you'll buy whatever supplies you need. If there's trouble, you leave it to me."

"We ain't afraid to fight," Jake said.

Clint looked at both men, who were in their twenties and looked competent enough.

"All right," he said. "If it comes to that, you keep your eyes on me. You don't move until I do. Is that understood by both of you?"

Jake nodded and Harry said, "Understood."

"Then let's go."

Traveling with the wagon, it took a bit over two hours to reach Bathurst. When they did, Clint fell in behind the wagon and followed them, since they knew the way.

They pulled the wagon to a stop in front of what looked to Clint like a general store. He didn't know what they called it in Australia.

"What's this place?" he asked.

"The general store," Jake said.

"Fine," Clint said, dismounting. "You see any of Collier's men around?"

"Don't know what they look like," Harry said.

"I guess we'll just have to wait for trouble to develop, then. Let's go inside and get what we need."

What "we" need? All Megan Forster had to do was bat her eyes and ask him, and already he was saying "we."

Hell, that wasn't true.

She'd done a lot more than just bat her eyes, and yet she

hadn't offered him anything but money.

Clint stood off to one side while the two men made their purchases. When they had everything they needed he told them to carry it out to the buckboard.

"Ain't you gonna help?" Harry asked. Some of the stuff appeared to be heavy.

"I'd like to keep my hands free, Harry, if that's all right with you?"

Harry looked at the gun on Clint's hip, said, "Sorry," and followed Jake out.

It took three trips out to the buckboard to get it loaded up and when they came out the third time, there were suddenly five men standing around the wagon.

"Look here, fellas," one of them said. "These look like two of those Forster boys."

All five men were of a kind, whether from Australia or America. Hardcases, paid to be bullies, and liking what they were paid to do. Each of them carried a rifle.

Harry and Jack stepped down off the boardwalk and then stopped. Clint stayed on the walk.

"Can we help you boys?" he asked.

"Now, it seems to me you're the ones needing help," the spokesman of the group said. He was about six feet tall, thin, with what appeared to be a three-day growth of black beard. "Some of that stuff looks heavy."

"We can handle it."

"Can you, now?"

"Put it on the wagon, fellas," Clint said to Jack and Harry.

They nodded and started forward, but as they passed two of the men one of them put his leg out and tripped Jake, who went down under the weight of his load.

Clint stepped off the boardwalk and backhanded the man before he could see it coming. It was a good blow, jarring the man's teeth and knocking him to the ground.

"Why you—" the spokesman said, but as he started to raise his rifle, he was suddenly looking down the barrel of Clint's gun.

"I hate like hell to draw this if I'm not going to use it," Clint said, "so I'm asking you real nice . . . give me an excuse."

The man's eyes were wide, because the gun had appeared in Clint's hand like magic.

"You're crazy," he said when he found his voice. "There's five of us."

"Drop your rifles or there'll be a lot less of you."

The other men were looking at the spokesman, obviously waiting for him to call their move.

"And you'll be the first, friend," Clint said to the spokesman. "Now it's up to you whether or not you die today."

They matched stares for a few moments, and then the man said, "You are crazy," but dropped his rifle.

One by one rifles dropped to the ground. Clint looked at the man he'd knocked down, who was still sitting on the ground with his rifle next to him where he'd dropped it.

"Kick them under the wagon," Clint ordered.

One by one the men obeyed.

"You, too," he told the man on the ground, "Now get up."

The man got up.

"Pick up those supplies and put them on the buckboard."

The man didn't even bother looking his leader's way, he just did as he was told.

"All right, now all of you, back away . . . way back, across the street."

The five men obeyed and were soon standing on the opposite side of the street.

"All right, Jake, Harry, let's get going."

Jake and Harry hurriedly climbed aboard the buckboard. Clint holstered his gun and mounted Duke, keeping his eyes on the men across the street.

As the buckboard started down the street he walked Duke over to where the men stood.

"Tell your boss that the Forster place, the men and the cattle are off limits to him and his. Tell him if he doesn't listen, I'll be out to see him . . . personally."

He gave them a small salute and then followed the buckboard out of town.

When he caught up to the buckboard Jake reined the team in.

"I ain't never seen anything like that in my life," he said to Clint.

"Me, neither," Harry said. "How can you take on five men like that?"

"They backed down, didn't they?"

"Well, sure, but why?" Harry asked. "There was five of them, all with guns, and you were the only one of us armed. Why'd they back down?"

"Men like that always do," Clint said. "You see, when it comes right to it, nobody ever wants to be the first to die."

"But . . . what would have happened if they hadn't backed down? What if they all tried to shoot?"

"I would have killed them."

Harry swallowed and looked at Jake, who said, "A-all of them?"

"What do you think?" Clint said.

Jake and Harry exchanged a glance that plainly said they didn't know what to think.

"Come on," Clint said, "let's get this stuff back to the ranch before they get brave and come after us."

THIRTY-THREE

When they got back to the ranch Jake and Harry drove the wagon around to the back, so they could unload whatever belonged in the kitchen. A man came up to Clint and took Duke from him, and Clint went inside.

Clint found Megan in her office, sitting with her left side to him.

"Megan?"

"How did it go?" she asked without looking at him.

"Not too bad."

"Any trouble?"

"Some, but we took care of it."

"Good."

"Your supplies are being unloaded. I think I'll just have to wait and see what happens as a result of what just occurred in town."

"You didn't . . . kill anyone, did you?"

"It wasn't necessary."

"That's good."

He found it odd that she hadn't faced him yet, but maintained that same position.

"Are you all right?"

"Yes," she said, her tone weary, "yes, I'm fine, Clint."

It was almost as if she didn't want him to see that side of her face.

"Megan—" he said, starting toward her.

"No, stay there!" she said.

"What's wrong? What happened?"

"Nothing serious," she said, "nothing. . . ."

He crossed the room and took her by the arm, turning her toward him. Her right eye had a swelling beneath it that was already starting to discolor.

"Who did that?" he demanded. "Did Jack come back?"

"No," she said, "no, it wasn't Jack."

"Pickett?" he asked.

"It's all right," she said, "really. He came in angry and we had an argument."

"He hit you."

"And I fired him"

"Where is he?"

"Gone by now."

He turned to leave, but she made a grab for his arm and caught his sleeve.

"Clint, don't," she said. "It's over, let it be."

Clint felt that the only thing worse than a backshooter was a man who beat women.

"It's not over," he said, "but I'll let it be . . . for now. Come on," he said, pulling her out of her chair, "let's get something for that eye."

"All right."

As they started for the door she said, "I'm glad you're back safely."

"I know," he said, "So am I."

The day passed without incident, with Clint for the most part roaming the grounds. He had Megan instruct some of the men to stand watch in shifts and let her know if anyone was approaching the ranch.

"Can I tell them that you're the new foreman?" she asked at one point.

"Hell, no," he said.

"Why not?"

"Because I'm not the foreman, Megan. Pick somebody from your men."

"Nobody would be as good as you."

"That's bull. I don't know the first thing about running a ranch. All I'm doing is trying to save it for you."

Single-handedly, he thought, like a fool who's let a woman talk him into something he shouldn't be involved in.

Now, as night started to fall, he wondered where Jack was and what he was doing. Would he be coming back tonight?

Going in for dinner, he found himself hoping that Jack wouldn't be returning tonight.

That would leave Clint and Megan in the house alone, except for the servants.

Who knew what would happen then?

THIRTY-FOUR

"Tell me about John Collier," Clint said at dinner.

There was only he and Megan, sitting at opposite ends of the table. He felt the distance between them was a necessity.

"What is there to tell?"

"When did he show up around here?"

"Several months ago. His land adjoins mine to the south and to the west."

"And he's trying to move in on you."

"Yes."

"Has he bought anyone else out?"

"There aren't that many places in the area, but he has been

staking some claims to land that's traditionally been open land."

"What kind of law do you have out here?"

"The kind you make yourself."

He nodded. He knew about that kind of law, he just didn't like being the one to hand it out.

"Do you think Jack will be back tonight?" she asked.

"I don't know. His original plan was to return tonight, but he had that look in his eye."

"What look?"

"The look that gold puts in people's eyes."

"Oh, that look."

She seemed to become ill at ease when the subject of gold came up. Or maybe it was the subject of Jack.

Come to think of it, sitting here with Jack's wife, the subject of Jack made him a little ill at ease, too.

"How's your eye?" he asked.

She touched it at the reminder and said, "It'll be all right."

"Swelling doesn't look too bad."

"Thanks."

"Did you really fire Pickett?"

"Yes."

"Before or after he hit you?"

"Before. Once I fired him and he was no longer my employee he seemed to feel that gave him the right to put his hands on me."

"What did you do?"

"I hit him . . . and then he hit me back, harder"

Clint felt that she was lying. He felt certain that she must have slept with Pickett on more than one occasion. Still, if she didn't want his hand on her on this occasion, that was her right.

"Have you argued before?"

"Yes."

"Have you ever fired him before?"

"No."

"I thought he was valuable to you?"

"I built this place without him, I can keep it going without him."

"I'm sure you can."

There was a long silence and then she said, "Unless you want the job."

"We talked about that this afternoon, Megan."

"We didn't really talk about it," she said. "We just sort of . . . skimmed over it."

"A skim was all the idea deserved," he said. "Besides, I'll be going back to America soon."

"How soon?"

He shrugged.

"You're not enjoying your stay in Australia?"

"It's not that," he said, although he wasn't. "It just hasn't solved anything for me. I feel the same." Especially since he was right back where he started from, poking his nose—and his gun—back into other people's business.

"What were you looking for?"

"Freedom," he said. "Someplace where nobody would know who I was."

"You should have left your gun home."

"What?"

"Your gun," she said. "You should have left it home. Carrying it with you meant you didn't really want to leave behind what you thought you wanted to leave behind."

He stared at her.

"Does that make any sense?" she asked.

He smiled.

"That makes a lot of sense, actually," he said, "a lot of sense."

"Well, then . . ."

"Well, then . . . what?"

"Put your gun away."

"If I did that," he said, "who would help you keep your ranch?"

She shrugged.

"If I'm meant to keep it, I'll keep it."

"No," he said. "I don't think that's the case. I think if you want something you have to make sure you get it, and if you have something you have to make sure you keep it."

Now she stared at him.

"Does that make any sense?" he asked.

She smiled.

"It makes a lot of sense, actually."

They finished dinner in silence, and then Clint went outside to look around.

THIRTY-FIVE

It was getting late and Clint was about to go back inside, when a man came running up to him.

"Mr. Adams?"

"Yeah," Clint said, trying to remember the man's name and failing.

"You'd better get over to the stable. There's some trouble."

"What kind of trouble—" Clint started to ask, but the man turned and ran back the way he came.

The only thing Clint could think of was that something had happened to Duke. He broke into a run.

He entered the stable and found that it was brightly lit. As he stepped inside, he heard the door shut behind him. Suddenly he knew he'd been duped.

He stood there and waited while they surrounded him. There were five of them, and the odd thing was that none of them were armed. The other odd thing was that they were all Megan's men.

"What's going on?" he asked.

"Somebody wants to see you," one of them said.

Clint was about to ask who, when Pickett stepped out from one of the stalls.

"What's going on Pickett?"

"I guess you know I've been fired," Pickett said.

"So I've heard."

"Don't think I don't know what happened."

"What did happen, Pickett?"

"You got rid of Jack and turned Megan to your favor. That meant that I had to go. I don't know how you convinced her, but you did."

"I didn't convince her of anything, Pickett. You did it yourself."

"I'm gonna give you a beating, Adams, and the only way you can avoid it is to shoot an unarmed man—with witnesses."

"Well, since there's hardly any law out here, Pickett, I don't think that would be a problem," Clint said, and for a moment he saw uncertainty in Pickett's eyes. However, when he dropped his gunbelt to the floor the man's eyes hardened once again.

"Now that's a mistake," Pickett said. "You should have killed me."

"And you should never have hit Megan, Pickett," Clint said. "I'm going to make you regret that."

The other men formed a circle around the two men.

Sizing up his opponent, Clint knew the man was larger and younger, but Clint thought that with the man's bulk he himself might be the faster of the two.

Pickett began to advance at him, his hands held widely apart. Clint circled, still weighing his advantages—which, admittedly, did not seem many.

He fell into a boxing stance, which did not faze the man, but when he threw a left jab into the man's face, hitting him squarely in the nose, Picketts reaction was one of obvious puzzlement. He obviously had not seen the blow coming.

Shaking off his confusion, the big man once again began to shuffle forward, and again Clint got him with a quick jab, and then another. The man's nose began to bleed. Clint decided to move quickly, while the man was still confused. He knew he was going to have to finish him fast, because he'd never outlast him if the fight went on much longer. He threw another jab and followed with a quick, crushing right—neither of which landed. The brave was apparently a quick study, and when Clint threw the jab he backed away from it. Consequently, when Clint threw the right he missed completely and threw himself off balance. Pickett balled up his right fist and threw it into Clint's right side. As Pickett's fist struck him a cry went up from the other men in the stable. The air went out of Clint's lungs and he staggered away from any follow-up blow.

Righting himself, he faced Pickett again and noticed that the man was looking very confident—certainly more confident than he himself felt.

Since the man had adjusted to Clint's boxing stance, Clint fell into a wrestler's crouch and advanced on the man. As Pickett threw another punch, Clint stepped inside of it and drove his shoulder into the man's midsection. From there he straightened up, bringing Pickett up off his feet and then throwing the man down on his back. The maneuver took a lot out of Clint, as the man was very heavy, and Pickett scrambled to his feet, showing more embarrassment than injury.

Clint felt he was in real trouble. He was going to have to do something desperate, if he could think of something.

He and Pickett circled each other for the next few moments, trading blows, some of which landed, some of which didn't. Clint felt that he was absorbing more damage than he was handing over.

Finally Clint figured he might as well go all-out. He launched a headlong dive and caught Pickett at the knees, driving him to the ground. He contrived to fall on the man with all his weight, and was rewarded when the man grunted in pain. His plan had been to get the man off his feet and onto the ground, where perhaps his superior wrestling skills would win out.

Pickett was quick, though, and he slid away from Clint before Clint could take advantage. Not only that, but once he was clear, the man threw a kick that caught Clint on the side of the jaw, making spots appear before his eyes. Now it was his turn to roll away and try to put some distance between himself and Pickett.

The men forming the circle were shouting and yelling now, calling out encouragement to their man. The side of Clint's face ached, but absorbing the kick had reminded him of something. Pickett was wearing shoes, and he was wearing Western boots. If he could land a similar kick, it would do much more damage than the one he'd just been hit with. Of course, that would mean getting the man off his feet again, and he wasn't going to accomplish that the same way twice.

Both men regained their feet and began circling again. Clint was aware of the burning sensation in his chest, and also that

Pickett still looked comparatively fresh.

Clint decided to use some patience, and maybe catch his breath. He continued to circle and feint, never really trying to land a telling blow. The Australian was patient, as well, but finally he ran out of patience before Clint did.

He shouted something at Clint and charged him. Clint allowed the man to run into him, absorbed the impact, and fell away with it, taking the man down with him. He slithered away from him once they hit the ground, then drew his boot back and let it fly with a kick.

Pickett was too quick for him. He caught Clint's foot and pushed it away, then leaped and landed on Clint's chest with all his weight.

Clint struggled beneath the man's weight, but his hands were pinned between them. Slowly, Pickett began to bring his hands up to Clint's throat, and when they closed around it, Clint knew he was very near death. As the man's hands squeezed tighter Clint began to see red spots before his eyes, but he still could not free his hands. Pickett's face was so close to his that the man's breath was harsh in his face. Finally in desperation, he brought his head forward as hard as he could, slamming his forehead into the man's. Pickett's forehead split, and he cried out. He released his hold on Clint's throat to reach for his head, and Clint heaved up off the ground, throwing Pickett off him.

Both men staggered to their feet, and Pickett was momentarily blinded by the blood flowing down from his head into his face. Clint seized the opportunity before it disappeared. He took a step foward and kicked Pickett viciously in the lower abdomen. The man bent over immediately, and Clint followed through with a swift kick to the jaw. Pickett staggered a moment, froze, and then fell to the ground.

He lay sprawled in the dirt, and suddenly all the noise that the observers had been making died down and it was deadly quiet.

Clint staggered a bit in his attempt to stay on his feet as he picked up his gunbelt.

"You men still want to work here?"

They all exchanged glances, and then alternately nodded and said, "Yes."

"Are you loyal to Mrs. Forster or to Pickett?"

"To Mrs. Forster," one of them said. "Mr. Adams, we owed Pickett—"

"Forget it," he said. "Just get him out of here and we'll forget this. Agreed?"

They all looked at each other, and then the spokesman said, "Agreed."

Clint staggered to the door, slipped out, and then leaned against it, catching his breath.

He fervently hoped he'd be able to make it to the house.

THIRTY-SIX

When Clint came back into the house, it was quiet. He assumed that Megan had gone to sleep long ago.

He went up the stairs to his room, wondering if he'd find little Jean waiting for him in his bed. When he didn't, he was glad. He didn't really feel up to entertaining her tonight.

He pulled off his shirt, gave up on his boots when a pain in his side kept him from pulling them off, and laid back on the bed.

A knock on the door woke him and he had no idea how long he'd been laying there. He tried to get up and groaned.

The knock was repeated and he tried getting up again, this time with more success. When he was upright, he actually didn't feel too bad—until he tried to walk.

The knock came again, followed by Megan's voice.

"Clint? Are you in there?"

"I'm here," he called out, making his way to the door and opening it.

"Jesus," Megan said.

"It's all right," he told her, "it looks worse than it feels."

"Well, it sure couldn't feel as bad as it looks or you'd be dead," Megan said.

He backed away and she entered, closed the door, and then she took his arm and led him back to the bed.

"I'll be right back," she said when she had him on the bed. "I'll have to get some hot water."

Megan took the pitcher from the dresser and left the room. She was back in about fifteen minutes with the water and a bottle of whiskey, and sat on the bed next to him.

"What happened?" she asked, taking his face in both hands so she could examine it.

"I had a fight."

"No kidding? Who with?"

"Pickett."

"Pike?" she said. "Clint, I asked you—"

"He came after me, Megan."

"Where?"

"In the livery."

"How did he get there?"

"He had some help. Apparently some of the men felt a loyalty to him."

"Who are they?" she asked. "I'll fire them tomorrow."

"Jeez," he said, "I don't think I'd be able to pick them out."

"Clint—"

"Come on, Megan. You can't afford to lose men right now."

She probed his torso, bringing several painful responses from him.

"You might have a broken rib."

"Or two."

"And then again, they might just be sore."

"I can tell you for sure that they're sore."

"How's your head feel?"

"Like hell."

She bathed his face, then helped him remove his shirt and bathed his torso. By the time she was done all of the dried blood had been removed, and the cuts were proven to be less than serious.

"Here, drink this," Megan said, handing him the bottle of whiskey. "I wasn't able to carry a glass."

"This is fine."

He took the bottle and drank deeply, starting a fire inside of him.

"How do you feel?" Megan asked.

"A lot better."

"Because I nursed you."

"No, because I had a drink . . . and I think I'll have another."

"Sure."

He took another swig and then handed the bottle back.

"Are you sure you're all right?"

"Yeah," he said, moving his arms and legs. "Surprisingly enough, I don't feel too bad. You are a good nurse."

"Not as good as I'm going to be," she said.

She stood up once again, this time to discard the dress. Her body was long and graceful, and her breasts were large and round, with brown nipples.

"Megan—"

"This is why I really came to your room, Clint," she said. "If you don't feel up to it, please tell me."

"No," he said, staring at her breasts, "no, I feel just fine."

"Fine enough to get your pants and boots off?" she asked, grinning.

As it turned out he needed her help a little, but finally he was naked on the bed.

"Megan—"

"Hush," she said. "You just rest and I'll do the hard work."

She touched his penis lightly with both hands, running her fingers over it, and he moaned.

"Did I hurt you?"

"Hell, no . . . "

She smiled, then leaned over and ran her tongue lovingly around the swollen tip of his penis. He moaned and she took the spongy head into her mouth, wetting it thoroughly.

"Can I get on the bed with you without hurting you?" she asked.

"I wish you would."

She went to the foot of the bed and crawled on that way, so that she could settle between his legs. She kissed his inner thighs, ran her tongue over his balls, and then from the base of his erection to the tip and back down again. He laid back with his eyes closed and surrendered himself to the sensations she was causing with her mouth.

She kissed his belly, laved his navel with her tongue, then ran her hair over his swollen penis, making him feel like he had a million nerve endings down there. She teased him with her tongue, running it up and down his length, and he lifted his hips in frustration. Finally, he felt the hot ring of her mouth descend on him, taking the swollen head, and then much of the shaft into her mouth. Slowly, her head began to bob up and down, and he felt one of her hands wrap around the base of his penis.

She sucked gently at first, and then with increasing ardor until she was moaning and he was lifting his hips in unison with her tempo. When he erupted into her mouth he groaned aloud, and she accommodated his entire emission without any problem, moaning her appreciation.

When she let him slide free of her mouth it was still erect and she said, "Let me know if I hurt you."

She eased up onto his hips, allowing her weight to rest on him little by little, until she was sitting heavily on him with his penis deep inside her.

"Hurt?" she asked.

"No," he lied, but whatever discomfort he was feeling as a result of his bruises was well worth it.

She began to slide up and down his rigid shaft, and he reached for her marvelous breasts, squeezing them in his hands. She moaned when he touched her and threw her head back, quickening her ride.

"Clint, oh Clint . . ." she groaned.

"Megan—"

He pulled her down so that he could suck her breasts, bite her nipples as she continued to ride him, and when he felt her begin to tremble he reached behind her, cupped her buttocks and moved her on him even faster. When she came she cried out, then cut off the cry by biting her lip. When he exploded inside of her she bit down on her lip to keep from yelling, then bit his shoulder. Her hair was fragrant on his face and he squeezed her buttocks as he continued to fill her.

Carefully, she rolled off of him and laid down next to him. She put her hand on his shoulder, the one she hadn't bitten and said, "Do you get bitten often?"

He remembered that Jean had bitten him, and he didn't know what to say.

She rubbed it and said, "Was it Jean?"

"Yes."

"I thought so. When I couldn't find her to draw my bath, and then she turned up . . . also I saw the way she was looking at you."

"You don't mind?"

"That I've shared you with a servant?" she asked, laughing. "No, I'm not that much of a snob."

"Thank God."

"But I don't think I'll feel so charitable from here on in," she said, touching his semi-erect penis.

"Megan—"

"I know," she said, "you need your rest. Go ahead, close your eyes. I'll just stay here with you and keep you . . . warm."

And she did.

THIRTY-SEVEN

In the morning she woke him with kisses, and then sat astride him again. He reached up and filled both hands with her breasts as she sat up straight on him. He thumbed the nipples while she swiveled her hips on him, as if she were trying to screw herself down on him even tighter. Her eyes were closed and her head was thrown back. He liked the way she looked, biting her lower lip like that. She reminded him of Jean, only she was heavier than the small girl.

"Oh, Clint, yes," she said, moving up and down on him now, "yes, yes. . . ."

She was bouncing on him now as her orgasm approached and he reached behind her, filling both hands with her ample buttocks. Dressed she had not look so fulsome. Now he saw that she really could become a big woman if she gave herself half a chance, but right now was built along very comfortable lines . . . lines that he wanted to take advantage of.

He lifted her off him, and while she was protesting, flipped her over onto her back.

"Just a change of position," he said.

"Won't it hurt?"

He smiled and said, "You or me?"

He mounted her and she opened her plump thighs so that he could drive into her.

"Oooh, Jesus, yes, you're splitting me. . . ."

He slid his hands beneath her, again cupping her buttocks, and began to drive into her quickly. She lifted her hips to him, grunting, wrapping her hands in the sheet, and then suddenly she was shuddering and moaning beneath him. He drove into her a few more times before he started spurting into her, and she moaned louder when she felt his hot seed filling her.

Over breakfast Megan asked, "What should we do about Collier?"

"I think maybe I'll go and see Mr. Collier."

"I'll come with you."

"No."

"Then take some of my men."

"No."

"You're not going to go alone."

"Yes, I am."

"You can't—"

"Don't you see? If I ride over there alone, it gives me an edge over him."

"I don't understand that at all," she said. "You'll be outnumbered."

"Technically speaking only," he said.

When Clint was leaving the house with intentions of heading for Collier's place, one of Megan's men came running up. It was not one of the men who had been in the barn the night before.

"Mr. Adams, Mrs. Forster," he said.

Megan was on the porch and said, "What is it, Kyle?"

"Somebody's coming."

"Who?" Clint asked.

"I don't know."

"How many?"

"About six altogether."

"All right," Clint said, turning to look up at Megan. "As they get close let me know if you recognize anyone."

She nodded, and they heard the sound of approaching hoofbeats.

Soon Clint saw the six riders who were approaching, and as they came closer Megan caught her breath.

"Collier?" he asked.

"Yes."

That was what he thought. He recognized the other men from town.

"Just stand easy, Megan."

Clint studied the man in the lead. He was a man in his fifties, with sandy hair and a sandy beard, slender almost to the point of being skinny.

"Mrs. Forster," Collier greeted as he reined in his horse. Behind him the five men fanned out, rifles in hand.

"Mr. Collier," Megan said. "What can I do for you?"

Instead of answering, Collier looked at Clint.

"You must be the gunman my men told me about."

"Gunman?" Clint said. "I don't know of any gunman here, Mr. Collier."

"Well, you're American, that's for certain."

"And proud of it."

"I would like to suggest that you go back home."

"I intend to," Clint said.

"Good—"

"Just as soon as the problem is resolved."

"And what problem is that?"

"Your harassment of Mrs. Forster, in an attempt to force her to sell."

"Force her to sell?" Collier asked, looking surprised. "I've made repeated offers, but I don't recall—"

"Cut the crap, Collier," Clint said. "Let's lay our cards on the table."

"Is that an American saying?" Collier asked.

"Up to now you've damaged fences, killed some cows, and beaten up some men, but you've never done any real damage."

"What do you call real damage?"

Clint waited a beat and then said, "You haven't killed anyone."

"And I don't intend to."

"Well, that's the only way you'll make me sell," Megan said.

"You mean if I kill one of your men, you'll sell?"

"No," she said, "you'll get my place only if you kill me."

"Mr. Collier," one of the men said. It was the same man who'd played spokesman in town. "Why don't you let us—"

"Shut up!" Collier said. "I don't pay you for advice."

The man tightened his lips and kept quiet, glaring at Clint.

Clint had made a snap decision about Collier, but he was fairly certain he was right. He did not think Collier had it in him to kill to get what he wanted. He thought the man would do anything short of that, which included hiring five bullies.

"Mr. Collier," Clint said, "while I've been here, I've discovered something about Australia."

"Which is?"

"It's very big," Clint said, "and there's plenty of land for the taking—so why do you want someone elses? Why can't you be content to have a good neighbor, rather than make enemies with your neighbor?"

"Young man," Collier said, "I did not get where I am today by making friends."

"Well, maybe you've missed something along the way."

"Mrs. Forster," Collier said, "I resent your bringing in an American gunman."

"I didn't bring Mr. Adams in," she said. "He's my husband's guest."

"Your husband?"

"Yes."

"I wasn't aware that you had a husband," Collier said. "At least, I thought he was dead."

"Yes, so did I," she said, "but he's back."

"I'd like to meet him."

Suddenly Clint had Collier pegged even better than he had thought before. The man didn't know how to talk to a woman, didn't know how to react to having a woman rancher as a neighbor. The sudden appearance of the man might have been what was needed to settle the problem.

"I'll have him come see you, Mr.Collier," Megan said, "as soon as he returns."

"Where has he gone?"

"He's been away from home for a long time," Clint said. "He's gone out to take a good long look at Australia. He'll be back soon."

"Jack Forster, isn't that his name?" Collier asked.

"Yes."

"I've heard of him," Collier said. "I'll look foward to meeting him."

Collier turned his horse and started away. Clint kept a wary eye on his hired bullies, and sure enough they weren't satisfied with the way things had gone.

As their spokesman brought his rifle up, Clint drew and shot him out of the saddle. One of the other men continued to raise his rifle, and Clint shot him as well. The man's rifle discharged into the ground as he fell off his horse.

The other three men were unsure as what to do until Collier shouted, "Don't shoot!"

Collier turned his horse again and looked down at his two dead men.

"You may not be willing to kill to take her land, Mr. Collier," Clint said, "but Mrs. Forster is willing to kill to keep it."

"So I see," Collier said. "Well, I'll have none of this. You men are all fired. Take your friends and get out."

The three of them dismounted, picked up their friends—one dead, one wounded—put them back on their horses, and led them away.

"Mrs. Forster, I'm sure your husband and I can work out our differences."

"I'm sure you can, Mr. Collier."

"I apologize for the behavior of my men to date."

Megan simply inclined her head, and Collier once again turned his horse and rode off. Clint holstered his gun and walked up the stairs to stand next to Megan, who was shaking.

"I don't think I really understand what happened," Clint said. "What did he mean that he's heard of Jack?"

"Jack didn't tell you? He's very famous here in Australia. He's killed crocodiles with a knife. He's something of a local legend."

"No," Clint said "He didn't mention the legend part."

"I'm surprised."

"So am I," Clint said. "He couldn't keep his mouth shut about my reputation, but he certainly did about his own."

Megan touched Clint's arm and said, "Let's go inside, Clint. I don't think I'll have any trouble with Collier anymore."

"You'll probably have to keep Jack around for a while."

"I guess I can take that," she said. "After all, he is my husband, and Pike is gone. I'll need a man to help run this place."

"Sounds like things might work out."

"And what about you?"

"Me?" he asked. "I think I'm going to head for home tomorrow morning, Megan."

"I thought you might," she said. "Why not wait for Jack to come back?"

"Well, if he comes back tonight I'll say good-bye, but I know the way back to Sydney, and I don't think I'll have any problem getting a boat—I mean, ship."

"Well," she said, "if he doesn't come back tonight, we'll have one more night together."

"I just had a thought," Clint said.

"What?"

"What if he doesn't come back at all?"

"He'll be back," she said. "He's looking for gold."

"So?"

"If he looks long enough he'll find it."

"You mean . . . there is gold out there?"

"Yes," she said, "but it's mine. You see, I already found it. That's how I was able to build this place up."

"You mean . . . you're rich?"

"Not rich, but pretty well off. It wasn't a big strike—"

"But there is one around here, then."

"Maybe," she said.

"And maybe Jack will find it."

"And maybe not," she said. "If not, he'll have to be satisfied with mine."

Clint marveled at the irony. Jack was looking all over the place for gold, when the whole time his wife had already found it. It was also ironic that it was Jack Forster's "legend" that would help solve the problem with John Collier.

"Come on," she said. "I'll show you my gold mine."

Watch for

THE MUSTANG HUNTERS

eighty-second novel in the
exciting GUNSMITH series

coming in October!

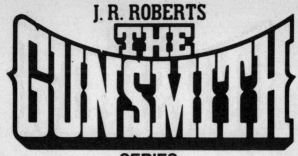

SERIES

Please send the titles I've checked above. Mail orders to:

BERKLEY PUBLISHING GROUP
390 Murray Hill Pkwy., Dept B
East Rutherford, NJ 07073

NAME _____

ADDRESS _____

CITY _____

STATE _____ ZIP _____

Please allow 6 weeks for delivery.
Prices are subject to change without notice.

POSTAGE & HANDLING:
$1.00 for one book, $.25 for each
additional. Do not exceed $3.50.

BOOK TOTAL	$_____
SHIPPING & HANDLING	$_____
APPLICABLE SALES TAX (CA, NJ, NY, PA)	$_____
TOTAL AMOUNT DUE	$_____

PAYABLE IN US FUNDS.
(No cash orders accepted.)

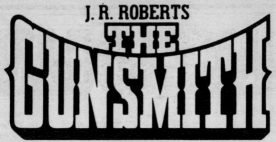

J. R. ROBERTS

THE GUNSMITH

SERIES

Please send the titles I've checked above. Mail orders to:

BERKLEY PUBLISHING GROUP
390 Murray Hill Pkwy., Dept. B
East Rutherford, NJ 07073

NAME _____

ADDRESS _____

CITY _____

STATE _____ ZIP _____

Please allow 6 weeks for delivery.
Prices are subject to change without notice.

POSTAGE & HANDLING:
$1.00 for one book, $.25 for each
additional. Do not exceed $3.50.

BOOK TOTAL	$_____
SHIPPING & HANDLING	$_____
APPLICABLE SALES TAX (CA, NJ, NY, PA)	$_____
TOTAL AMOUNT DUE	$_____

PAYABLE IN US FUNDS.
(No cash orders accepted.)

JAKE LOGAN

___	0-425-09342-5	RAWHIDE JUSTICE	$2.50
___	0-425-09395-6	SLOCUM AND THE INDIAN GHOST	$2.50
___	0-425-09567-3	SLOCUM AND THE ARIZONA COWBOYS	$2.75
___	0-425-09647-5	SIXGUN CEMETERY	$2.75
___	0-425-09896-6	HELL'S FURY	$2.75
___	0-425-10016-2	HIGH, WIDE AND DEADLY	$2.75
___	0-425-09783-8	SLOCUM AND THE WILD STALLION CHASE	$2.75
___	0-425-10116-9	SLOCUM AND THE LAREDO SHOWDOWN	$2.75
___	0-425-10188-6	SLOCUM AND THE CLAIM JUMPERS	$2.75
___	0-425-10419-2	SLOCUM AND THE CHEROKEE MANHUNT	$2.75
___	0-425-10347-1	SIXGUNS AT SILVERADO	$2.75
___	0-425-10489-3	SLOCUM AND THE EL PASO BLOOD FUED	$2.75
___	0-425-10555-5	SLOCUM AND THE BLOOD RAGE	$2.75
___	0-425-10635-7	SLOCUM AND THE CRACKER CREEK KILLERS	$2.75
___	0-425-10701-9	SLOCUM AND THE RED RIVER RENEGADES	$2.75
___	0-425-10758-2	SLOCUM AND THE GUNFIGHTER'S GREED	$2.75
___	0-425-10850-3	SIXGUN LAW	$2.75
___	0-425-10889-9	SLOCUM AND THE ARIZONA KIDNAPPERS	$2.95
___	0-425-10935-6	SLOCUM AND THE HANGING TREE	$2.95
___	0-425-10984-4	SLOCUM AND THE ABILENE SWINDLE	$2.95
___	0-425-11233-0	BLOOD AT THE CROSSING	$2.95
___	0-425-11056-7	SLOCUM AND THE BUFFALO HUNTERS (On sale October '88)	$2.95
___	0-425-11194-6	SLOCUM AND THE PREACHER'S DAUGHTER (On sale November '88)	$2.95

Please send the titles I've checked above. Mail orders to:

BERKLEY PUBLISHING GROUP
390 Murray Hill Pkwy., Dept. B
East Rutherford, NJ 07073

POSTAGE & HANDLING:
$1.00 for one book, $.25 for each
additional. Do not exceed $3.50.

NAME_____

ADDRESS_____

CITY_____

STATE_____ZIP_____

Please allow 6 weeks for delivery.
Prices are subject to change without notice.

BOOK TOTAL	$_____
SHIPPING & HANDLING	$_____
APPLICABLE SALES TAX (CA, NJ, NY, PA)	$_____
TOTAL AMOUNT DUE	$_____
PAYABLE IN US FUNDS. (No cash orders accepted.)	

**The hard-hitting, gun-slinging
Pride of the Pinkertons is riding solo
in this new action-packed series.**

J.D. HARDIN'S

RAIDER

Sharpshooting Pinkertons Doc and Raider are
legends in their own time, taking care of outlaws
that the local sheriffs can't handle. Doc has
decided to settle down and now Raider takes on
the nastiest vermin the Old West has to offer
single-handedly...charming the ladies along the way.

__0-425-10757-4	**TIMBER WAR #10**	$2.75
__0-425-10851-1	**SILVER CITY AMBUSH #11**	$2.75
__0-425-10890-2	**THE NORTHWEST RAILROAD WAR #12**	$2.95
__0-425-10936-4	**THE MADMAN'S BLADE #13**	$2.95
__0-425-10985-2	**WOLF CREEK FEUD #14**	$2.95

Please send the titles I've checked above. Mail orders to:

BERKLEY PUBLISHING GROUP
390 Murray Hill Pkwy., Dept. B
East Rutherford, NJ 07073

NAME_____

ADDRESS_____

CITY_____

STATE_____ ZIP_____

Please allow 6 weeks for delivery.
Prices are subject to change without notice.

POSTAGE & HANDLING:
$1.00 for one book, $.25 for each
additional. Do not exceed $3.50.

BOOK TOTAL	$_____
SHIPPING & HANDLING	$_____
APPLICABLE SALES TAX (CA, NJ, NY, PA)	$_____
TOTAL AMOUNT DUE	$_____

PAYABLE IN US FUNDS.
(No cash orders accepted.)